英美经典诗歌选译

高 远 /译

海峡出版发行集团 | 福建教育出版社

图书在版编目（CIP）数据

英美经典诗歌选译/高远译. —福州：福建教育出版社，2022.5
ISBN 978-7-5334-9326-4

Ⅰ.①英… Ⅱ.①高… Ⅲ.①诗集－英国②诗集－美国 Ⅳ.①I12

中国版本图书馆CIP数据核字（2022）第070543号

Yingmei Jingdian Shige Xuanyi
英美经典诗歌选译
高　远　译

出版发行	福建教育出版社
	（福州市梦山路27号　邮编：350025　网址：www.fep.com.cn
	编辑部电话：0591-83786915　83779650
	发行部电话：0591-83721876　87115073　010-62024258）
出 版 人	江金辉
印　　刷	福建东南彩色印刷有限公司
	（福州市金山工业区　邮编：350002）
开　　本	890毫米×1240毫米　1/32
印　　张	11.75
字　　数	254千字
插　　页	2
版　　次	2022年5月第1版　2022年5月第1次印刷
书　　号	ISBN 978-7-5334-9326-4
定　　价	35.00元

如发现本书印装质量问题，请向本社出版科（电话：0591-83726019）调换。

前　言

　　诗歌是文学宝库中一颗璀璨的明珠。诗人们凭借其天赋，结合内容与形式，用富于音乐性的语言，创作出诗歌这一人间瑰宝。英语诗歌有着一千五百多年的历史，在古代、近现代和当代都产生了很多名篇佳作。这些佳作不仅是英语民族的文化遗产，而且也是全人类的精神财富。

　　《英美经典诗歌选译》涵盖英美两国许多优秀诗歌作品，全书共选英美古代、近代和当代四十位诗人，其中有古英语时代的英国诗人杰弗里·乔叟，也有当代美国诗坛的重要诗人塞尔维亚·普拉斯，他们是英美文学史上各个诗歌流派的代表性诗人。英诗有其自身诸多文体特点，如格律和音韵表现出的音乐美、传情达意的意境美以及诗体的形式美等。本书中包括各学派的典型代表作，配以文前导读与文后鉴赏，将极大丰富读者对英文诗歌的认识。

　　美学家朱光潜曾经说过，诗是文学的精华，一切纯文学都有诗的特质，好的艺术都是诗。他反复强调，想要培养纯正的文学趣味，最好从诗入手；能欣赏诗，自然能欣赏小说、散文、戏剧等。他还认为，研究诗歌是研究一般文学的最好的入门训练。在诗歌里摸索得到门径，再进一步研究其他种类文学，就不难了。他从自身的经验总结出：研究诗歌并非语言、文学的终极训练，而应是入门时必需的训练。这一总结不仅针对中文学习者，而且也适用于英语学习者。对英语学习者来说，诗歌学习对提高英语水平大有裨益。正如中国孩子进行中文启蒙教育时背《唐诗三百首》一样，英语学习者从初始阶段学英语诗歌，会在潜移默化中提高文学鉴赏水平。

高　远

2021年10月

目 录

杰弗里·乔叟
  《坎特伯雷故事集》开篇（选段）/ 1
托马斯·怀特
  久久爱恋是我思念的港湾 / 7
亨利·霍华德
  统治我并活在我思念中的爱 / 11
埃德蒙·斯宾塞
  《仙后》第一卷序 / 15
威廉·莎士比亚
  《莎士比亚十四行诗集》第18首 / 21
  《莎士比亚十四行诗集》第116首 / 25
托马斯·坎皮恩
  有一座花园在她的脸上 / 29
无名氏
  《圣咏集》第23首 / 35
约翰·多恩
  离别赠言：莫伤悲 / 39
  《神圣十四行诗》第10首 / 45

本·琼生
　　献给西莉亚的歌（上）/ 49
　　献给西莉亚的歌（下）/ 53

罗伯特·赫里克
　　致少女：珍惜时光 / 57

乔治·赫伯特
　　美德 / 61

约翰·弥尔顿
　　祈求神助（选自《失乐园》）/ 65

安妮·布拉德斯特里特
　　致我亲爱的丈夫 / 71

安德鲁·马维尔
　　致羞怯的情人 / 75

爱德华·泰勒
　　我是生存的面包——沉思录之八 / 81

托马斯·格雷
　　墓园挽歌 / 87

威廉·布莱克
　　老虎 / 103
　　伦敦 / 109

威廉·华兹华斯
　　我像一朵云孤独地漫游 / 113

塞缪尔·泰勒·柯勒律治
　　忽必烈汗或梦中幻影 / 119

珀西·比希·雪莱
　　西风颂 / 127
约翰·济慈
　　夜莺颂 / 139
　　希腊古瓮颂 / 149
　　致秋天 / 157
拉尔夫·瓦尔多·爱默生
　　康科德之歌 / 163
　　梵天 / 167
　　日子 / 171
亨利·沃兹沃斯·朗费罗
　　生命的礼赞 / 175
埃德加·爱伦·坡
　　致海伦 / 181
　　安娜贝尔·李 / 185
阿尔弗雷德·丁尼生
　　雄鹰 / 191
　　过沙洲 / 195
罗伯特·布朗宁
　　夜里相会 / 199
　　早上分别 / 203
　　我已故的公爵夫人 / 207
沃尔特·惠特曼
　　我歌唱自己 / 215
　　自己之歌 / 219

啊，船长！我的船长！/ 223

马修·阿诺德

多佛海滩 / 229

艾米莉·狄金森

我是无名之辈！你是谁？ / 235

这是我给世人的信 / 239

我死时听苍蝇嗡叫 / 243

说出全部真理而不直说 / 247

我临终前已经死过两回 / 251

托马斯·哈代

黑暗中的鸫鸟 / 255

啊，是你正在我的坟上刨？ / 261

阿尔弗列德·爱德华·霍斯曼

树最可爱唯樱花 / 267

当我二十一岁时 / 271

威廉·巴特勒·叶芝

第二次圣临 / 275

驶向拜占庭 / 281

罗伯特·弗罗斯特

雪夜林边小憩 / 287

未选择的路 / 291

修墙 / 297

华莱士·史蒂文斯

雪人 / 303

冰淇淋皇帝 / 307

威廉·卡洛斯·威廉斯

　　春天与万物 / 311

　　要说的就是这 / 317

希尔达·杜丽特尔

　　海玫瑰 / 321

　　山林仙女 / 325

　　海伦 / 329

托马斯·斯特尔那斯·艾略特

　　J.阿尔弗瑞德·普鲁弗洛克的情歌 / 333

爱德华·埃斯特林·肯明斯

　　孤（一 / 349

　　无题 / 353

哈特·克兰

　　第二次远航 / 357

塞尔维亚·普拉斯

　　镜子 / 363

译后记 / 367

《坎特伯雷故事集》开篇(选段)
杰弗里·乔叟 著

导读:

《坎特伯雷故事集》(*The Canterbury Tales*)是英国诗人杰弗里·乔叟(Geoffrey Chaucer, 1343—1400)的一部诗歌体短篇小说集,包括30个朝圣者,其中有骑士、僧尼、商人、工匠、医生、律师、学者、农夫、家庭主妇等英国社会各阶层的人。他们聚在泰巴旅店,准备前往坎特伯雷朝拜圣托马斯。店主喜欢热闹,自告奋勇为他们当向导,提议在往返途中每人讲两个故事,以排解途中的寂寞,并当裁判选出讲故事最好的人,回店后大家一起请他吃饭。众人接受店主的建议,于是次日一同踏上朝圣旅途,开始讲故事。本文选自《英美诗歌名篇选读》(第二版),黄宗英编,高等教育出版社,2014年版,原文略有修改。

The General Prologue from The Canterbury Tales

Whan that Aprille with his shoures soote
The droughte of March hath perced to the roote,
And bathed every veyne in swich licour
Of which vertu engendred is the flour;
Whan Zephirus eek with his sweete breeth
Inspired hath in every holt and heeth
The tendre croppes, and the yonge sonne
Hath in the Ram his halfe cours yronne,
And smale foweles maken melodye,
That slepen al the nyght with open ye,
So priketh hem Nature in hir corages,
Thanne longen folk to goon on pilgrimages
And palmeres for to seken straunge strondes
To ferne halwes, kowthe in sondry londes;
And specially, from every shires ende
Of Engelond to Caunterbury they wende,
The hooly blisful martir for to seke
That hem hath holpen, whan that they were seeke.

那个四月带着绵绵春雨,
浸透了三月干旱的土地,
沐浴着植物每一根经络,
雨后之花显出生机勃勃;
西风携带着甜蜜的气息,
吹遍每一片森林和土地,
吹动每一片新鲜的树叶,
一年之初已过半个季节。
鸟儿唱起了美妙的曲调,
一整夜都睁着眼睛睡觉,
于是激起了香客的本性,
他们排一长队前去朝圣。
香客们为前往圣地膜拜,
面对神龛感知各种心态;
他们来自英国东西南北,
结伴而行前往坎特伯雷,
神圣殉道者为寻找幸福,
找到幸福是其已有所图。

Bifil that in that season on a day,
In Southwerk, at the Tabard, as I lay
Ready to go on pilgrimage and start
To Caunterbury, full devout at heart,
At night was came into that hostelrye
Wel nine and twenty in a company
Of sundry folk, by aventure yfalle
In fellowship, and pilgrims were they all
That toward Caunterbury town would ride.
The rooms and stables spacious were and wide,
And well we there were eased, and of the best.
And shortly, when the sonne was to reste,
So had I spoken with them, every one,
That I was of their fellowship anon,
And made agreement that weQ'd early rise
To take the road, as I will to you apprise.

But nathelees, whilst I have time and space,
Before yet further in this tale I pace;
It seems to me in accord with reason
To describe to you the state of every one
Of each of them, as it appeared to me,
And who they were, and what was their degree,
And even what clothes they were dressed in;
And with a knight thus will I first begin.

故事发生在那季的一日,
我在桥南泰巴旅馆歇息,
满怀着拳拳赤心的虔诚,
准备前往坎特伯雷朝圣,
二十九个香客组成一队,
住进那旅馆时夜色渐黑,
这些香客来自各行各业,
不期而遇结伴在此过夜。
他们次日都将骑着马匹,
前往坎特伯雷城朝圣去。
客房和马厩都十分宽敞,
我们大家住得无比舒畅。
没过多久当太阳西下时,
我即与他们相识并交谈,
大家约定好一大早起床,
而我会通知你们把路上。

然而在我讲这篇故事前,
我得占用你们一点时间,
这在我看来似乎有必要
将诸位情况向你们介绍,
描述每个人的职业归类,
各自身份及其社会地位,
甚至描述其穿着的服饰,
那么现在我就先说骑士。

鉴赏：

乔叟被公认为是中世纪英国最伟大的诗人之一，也是英诗的奠基人。其诗歌创作成熟期的作品《坎特伯雷故事集》，在内容和技巧上都达到其创作顶峰，是英国文学史上现实主义诗歌的典范。故事集虽只有21个完整故事和另一些未完成的片段，却包括当时欧洲多数文学题材，如骑士故事、市井故事、悲剧故事、喜剧故事、传奇、圣徒传、历史传说、宗教故事、动物寓言、宗教寓言、布道词等，堪称文学题材之宝库。乔叟把悲剧故事题材引入英国文学尤具特殊意义。

乔叟不仅创作出享誉世界的作品，而且还开辟了英国文学的新时代，为伊丽莎白时代英语文学的全面繁荣奠定基础，莎士比亚等后来者是乔叟时代探索与创新的最大受益者。他首创的英雄双韵体为以后的英国诗人所广泛采用。在同时代的主要英国文学家中，乔叟受外来影响无疑最为广泛，但从英国文学发展史的角度看，他又最具"英国性"，因而被誉为"英国诗歌之父"。

《坎特伯雷故事集》的艺术成就很高：作品将幽默和讽刺结合，喜剧色彩浓厚；人物形象鲜明，语言生动活泼，富有伦敦方言的生命力；作品展现广阔的社会画面，书中出现的香客来自社会各个阶层；作品综合采用中世纪各种文学体裁；总序和开场白中对人物描写和故事本身饶有趣味；作品的语言带有讲述人自身的特征，每人所讲的故事都体现出讲述人的身份、趣味、爱好、职业和生活经验。

久久爱恋我思念的港湾

托马斯·怀特 著

导读：

  托马斯·怀特（Thomas Wyatt，1503—1542）的突出贡献在于把十四行诗从意大利引入英国。1527年，他来到意大利，在首次接触十四行诗时，便被它的魅力深深吸引，继而开始翻译彼特拉克十四行诗，从此十四行诗开启在英国的传播。怀特译诗虽为兴起所致，却给英国诗歌的发展送去一缕春风。在《久久爱恋我思念的港湾》(*The Long Love That in My Thought Doth Harbor*)中，诗人把追求恋人比作一场旷日持久的战争，把爱恋比作自己的主人，从侍从的角度观察爱情的行动。

The Long Love That in My Thought Doth Harbor

The long love, that in my thought doth harbor,
And in mine heart doth keep his residence,
Into my face presseth with bold pretence,
And therein campeth displaying his banner.
She that me learneth to love and to suffer,
And wills that my trust, and lust's negligence
Be reined by reason, shame, and reverence,
With his hardiness taketh displeasure.
Wherewith love to the heart's forest he fleeth,
Leaving his enterprise with pain and cry,
And there him hideth, and not appeareth.
What may I do, when my master feareth,
But in the field with him to live and die?
For good is the life, ending faithfully.

久久爱恋我思念的港湾,
爱的居所就留在我心中,
爱的大胆借口烙我脸孔,
爱的旗帜在营地上招展。
爱教我动情也教我受难,
而欲望之过与诚信之用
既受理性也受羞畏之控,
以坚韧意志将坏事承担。
爱意飞入我内心的森林,
我不思慕爱时放声大哭,
将爱藏那让其不动声色。
主人惧怕时我能做什么:
在旷野上与爱生死相处?
生命永远在忠诚中结束。

鉴赏：

怀特是英国文艺复兴时期诗歌先行者之一，其主要贡献在于让英语语言文学化，使得英语文学不再逊色于其他欧洲语言。其许多作品译自或仿自意大利诗人彼特拉克的十四行诗，或仿自塞内卡和贺拉斯的某些诗作。诗人自己也创作过部分十四行诗。

在内容题材上，怀特的十四行诗未能摆脱彼特拉克的窠臼，他的一些诗作以爱情的试练为主题，讲述痴情的追求者与冷酷无情的情人的故事。在表现手法上，其爱情诗中灵动的想象和复杂的比喻为17世纪玄学诗派发先声。有些作品揶揄和讽刺当时都铎王朝的廷臣欲求晋升所表现出的伪善和逢迎。在韵律上，怀特的十四行诗富有极大的创新：彼特拉克十四行诗的前八句为abbaabba的韵式，后六句则为无定韵式；怀特继承彼特拉克前八句的韵式，但后六句则为cddcee的韵式。这一做法开英国十四行诗格式（三段四句加结尾对句）之先河。在诗歌体裁上，怀特做过多种尝试：如回旋诗、语录诗、连锁韵、八行诗、讽刺诗、单韵诗、三联叠句、换韵不等长四句、带重唱尾句的四句、法国式十二行诗和三十行诗。此外，他还开创一种名为保尔特的韵律——交替使用十二音节句（亚历山大诗行）和十四音节句，因此他被称为四音步抑扬格大师。

统治我并活在我思念中的爱

亨利·霍华德 著

导读：

亨利·霍华德（Henry Howard, 1517—1547）的《统治我并活在我思念中的爱》(*Love, That Doth Reign and Live within My Thought*) 是英国文艺复兴时期十四行诗的代表作之一。那时，十四行诗常表达男主人公爱而不得、备受煎熬的主题。这既是受中世纪骑士爱情诗的影响，也是刻意地矫揉造作。不同的是，这首诗有一种阳刚之美。诗中的军事用语一开始就营造出刚劲的气氛，最后的对句更表达出爱情至上的理想。作为权臣和武将的霍华德虽然早已被人遗忘，可是作为诗人的他及其诗作却为后世所铭记。

Love, That Doth Reign and Live within My Thought

Love, that doth reign and live within my thought,
And built his seat within my captive breast,
Clad in arms wherein with me he fought,
Oft in my face he doth his banner rest.
But she that taught me love and suffer pain,
My doubtful hope and eke my hot desire
With shamefast look to shadow and refrain,
Her smiling grace converteth straight to ire.
And coward Love, then, to the heart apace
Taketh his flight, where he doth lurk and plain,
His purpose lost, and dare not show his face.
For my lord's guilt thus faultless bide I pain,
Yet from my lord shall not my foot remove:
Sweet is the death that taketh end by love.

统治我并活在我思念中的爱，
在我被俘获的心中筑其阵地，
爱的盔甲在那与我交火开来，
常在我脸庞上插上爱的旗帜。
可她既教我爱也教我忍受苦，
要以胆怯的样子克制并遮掩
我难料的愿望与炽热的爱慕，
她优雅的笑脸顷刻转现怒颜。
这时胆怯的爱迅速飞回心中，
爱确实潜伏在那儿大发牢骚，
未达目的爱不敢露出其面容，
爱在为主人的过失备受煎熬，
却依然与它的主人步步相随：
以被爱而告终才是死得甜美。

鉴赏：

  亨利·霍华德在英国文学史上首创无韵诗，他把维吉尔的《埃涅伊德》第二卷和第四卷改编成五步抑扬格诗，并与托马斯·怀特爵士把十四行诗引入英国，为英国诗歌的伟大时期奠定基础。

  霍华德大部分的诗是在囚禁期间写就，他几乎所有的诗都在其去世后10年的1557年首度发表。他承认韦艾特为一代大师，并追随后者采用意大利诗的格式写英语诗。他把韦艾特译过的彼特拉克十四行诗又重译一遍，相比之下，他的翻译更为流畅、有气势，对英国十四行诗的发展起到重要作用。他最先发展莎士比亚采用的十四行诗形式。

  在其他短诗方面，霍华德不仅描写都铎王朝早期寻常的爱情和死亡主题，也描述伦敦生活、友谊和年轻人的生活。

《仙后》第一卷序

埃德蒙·斯宾塞 著

导读：

埃德蒙·斯宾塞（Edmund Spenser，1552—1599）是英国文艺复兴时期的伟大诗人。其代表作《仙后》（*The Faerie Queene*）是一部重要的宗教、政治史诗。诗人采取中世纪常用的讽喻传奇的形式，原定写12卷，却只完成6卷和第7卷的一部分，共约35000行。该诗以亚瑟王追求仙后格罗丽亚娜为引子，讲述仙后每年在宫中举行12天宴会，每天派一名骑士解除灾难，亚瑟王参与每个骑士冒险行动的故事。此处节选的《仙后》第1卷序采用新十四行诗格律：每节9行，前8行每行均10音节，第9行有12音节，按 ababbcbcc 形式押韵，这种形式被称作"斯宾塞诗节"（the Spenserian stanza）。

The Faerie Queene
The First Book

Lo I the man, whose Muse whilome did maske,
    As time her taught, in lowly Shepheards weeds,
    Am now enforst a far unfitter taske,
    For trumpets sterne to chaunge mine Oaten reeds,
    And sing of Knights and Ladies gentle deeds;
    Whose prayses having slept in silence long,
    Me, all too meane, the sacred Muse areeds
    To blazon broad emongst her learned throng:
Fierce warres and faithfull loues shall moralize my song.

Helpe then, O holy Virgin chiefe of nine,
    Thy weaker Novice to performe thy will,
    Lay forth out of thine everlasting scryne
    The antique rolles, which there lye hidden still,
    Of Faerie knights and fairest Tanaquill,
    Whom that most noble Briton Prince so long
    Sought through the world, and suffered so much ill,
    That I must rue his undeserved wrong:

你瞧我这个戴着面具的诗神,
　　时光教她穿低廉的牧人草衣,
　　我如今承当的职责更难胜任:
　　要用厉声小号替换我的牧笛,
　　歌颂骑士和贵妇的高尚事迹;
　　我的赞誉在寂寂无声中长眠,
　　神圣缪斯给平庸的我以昭示,
　　在她的博学人群中广为称赞:
我的诗歌将教化于忠爱与激战。

那么救救我吧纯洁至尊女神,
　　你的虚弱小鸟履行你的旨意,
　　拉出你一箱千秋不朽的古书,
　　古书卷里仍有精灵骑士藏匿,
　　还有塔娜奎尔最优雅的风姿,
　　最高贵的英国王子久久寻找,
　　寻遍世界却遭受如此多病疾,
　　以致我定为他做错之处懊恼:

17

O helpe thou my weake wit, and sharpen my dull tong.

And thou most dreaded impe of highest Jove,
    Faire Venus sonne, that with thy cruell dart
    At that good knight so cunningly didst rove,
    That glorious fire it kindled in his hart,
    Lay now thy deadly Heben bow apart,
    And with thy mother milde come to mine ayde:
    Come both, and with you bring triumphant Mart,
    In loves and gentle jollities arrayd,
After his murdrous spoiles and bloudy rage allayd.

And with them eke, O Goddesse heavenly bright,
    Mirrour of grace and Maiestie divine,
    Great Lady of the greatest Isle, whose light
    Like Phoebus lampe throughout the world doth shine,
    Shed thy faire beames into my feeble eyne,
    And raise my thoughts too humble and too vile,
    To thinke of that true glorious type of thine,
    The argument of mine afflicted stile:
The which to heare, vouchsafe, O dearest dred a-while.

敝人不才甘愿助你将钝钳磨好。

而你是最高天神最恐怖的后代,
　　维纳斯英俊之子用你残酷飞镖,
　　向那优秀骑士如此灵巧投过来,
　　飞镖在他心中燃起荣光的火苗,
　　这时你致命的檀弩却不及目标,
　　于是你温柔的母亲来向我求助:
　　你携得意洋洋的玛特一起来到,
　　我们在友爱的快乐中和睦相处,
缓和了残忍的掠夺和血腥的愤怒。

啊!与其勉强度日的聪明天女,
　　既是一面庄严高雅的神圣明镜,
　　也是最大岛屿的最杰出的女性,
　　其光芒如太阳神灯为世间照明,
　　请往我的倦眼里撒入靓丽光影,
　　提升我自身谦逊却卑劣的才思,
　　以便我想到你真正荣耀的原型,
　　对于我那令人折磨的低劣诗词:
　　啊!又爱又恨的天神请倾听一时。

鉴赏：

斯宾塞是从杰弗里·乔叟到莎士比亚之间的最杰出诗人。在以菲利普·锡德尼爵士（Sir Philip Sidney）为代表的英国创新诗人的影响下，1579年斯宾塞创作并发表了《牧人月历》（The Shephearde's Calender）。他还著有长诗《克劳茨回家记》（Colin Clouts Come Home Again），十四行诗集《小爱神》（Amoretti），《婚曲》（Epithalamion）等。1580年，他去爱尔兰，居住在女王赐给他的城堡里，在那里其代表作《仙后》（The Faerie Queene）于1590—1596年写作出版。

斯宾塞早在1569年就翻译过法国诗人杜倍雷的诗歌，并通过法文转译意大利诗人彼特拉克的诗歌。他最早的诗作《牧人月历》仿照罗马诗人维吉尔的古代牧歌。其重要作品《仙后》，用词华丽、情感细腻、格律严谨、优美动听。

从思想内容说，斯宾塞既有人文主义者对生活的热爱，也有新柏拉图主义的神秘思想，还带有清教徒的伦理宗教观念和强烈的资产阶级爱国情绪。他在诗歌形式方面一向乐于探索，在《仙后》诗里找到一种适用于长诗的格律形式，被称为"斯宾塞诗节"，拜伦、雪莱等诗人都沿用过。无论在思想上、语言上、诗歌艺术上，斯宾塞对后世英国诗人有深远的影响。他主要启发了马洛，使十音节诗行在无韵诗体里臻于完美，也影响到18世纪前期浪漫主义诗人汤姆逊、格雷以及19世纪浪漫主义诗人雪莱和济慈。

《莎士比亚十四行诗集》第18首

威廉·莎士比亚 著

导读：

威廉·莎士比亚（William Shakespeare，1564—1616）所处的英国伊丽莎白时代是爱情诗的盛世，写十四行诗更是一种时髦。莎士比亚无疑是那个时代的佼佼者，其十四行诗流传至今，魅力不减。他的诗一扫当时诗坛矫揉造作、绮艳轻糜、空虚无力的风气。有人评价说，他的诗是专业的文学创作。

Sonnet 18

Shall I compare thee to a summer's day?

Thou art more lovely and more temperate:

Rough winds do shake the darling buds of May,

And summer's lease hath all too short a date:

Sometime too hot the eye of heaven shines,

And often is his gold complexion dimm'd;

And every fair from fair sometime declines,

By chance or nature's changing course untrimm'd;

But thy eternal summer shall not fade

Nor lose possession of that fair thou ow'st;

Nor shall Death brag thou wander'st in his shade,

When in eternal lines to time thou grow'est:

So long as men can breathe or eyes can see,

So long lives this and this gives life to thee.

我欲把君比夏日,
君更可爱更温婉。
五月娇蕾狂风移,
夏日光阴何其短。
天眼时开炎炎热,
金色脸庞常暗淡;
群芳众艳终凋落,
时运天道褪芳颜;
可君长夏永无尽,
亦无逝去君娇容;
死神自夸随其影,
不朽诗篇伴君旁。
人要能活眼能明,
此诗长存赐君命。

爱德华·蒙克

《雨》

《莎士比亚十四行诗集》第116首

威廉·莎士比亚 著

导读：

  莎士比亚的第116首十四行诗阐释爱情的定义：爱情是永恒不变的。在诗人看来，真爱由两人构成，爱情虽像百合般纯洁而神圣，但只有为人们享受才能真正将它的美发挥得淋漓尽致；若爱情像神般可望而不可即，那么其即便再美丽再圣洁，也很难让人理解其真谛；爱情如果不能形成心中的共鸣，那么它的美就不能真正实现；爱情的核心为今生的共享与愉悦，需要两人共同呵护，而只有两者彼此忠诚，坚定不移，那么这样的爱才是真正的爱。爱情在变与不变中抉择，人们也在变与不变的矛盾中徘徊，并最终在此矛盾中取得爱的真经。

Sonnet 116

Let me not to the marriage of true minds
Admit impediments. Love is not love
Which alters when it alteration finds,
Or bends with the remover to remove:
O no! it is an ever-fixed mark
That looks on tempests and is never shaken;
It is the star to every wand'ring bark,
Whose worth's unknown, although his height be taken.
Love's not Time's fool, though rosy lips and cheeks
Within his bending sickle's compass come:
Love alters not with his brief hours and weeks,
But bears it out even to the edge of doom.
If this be error and upon me proved,
I never writ, nor no man ever loved.

我不认同此情形：
真心结发有障碍。
说变就变非真情，
见风使舵非真爱，
爱是永恒航标灯！
守望风暴不动摇；
迷途小舟引航星，
航标虽低价何标。
真爱非为时光愚，
红颜虽遭风雨扰；
爱经时光不扭曲，
而是持久到地老。
人若证明此为假，
无诗无人真爱过。

鉴赏：

莎士比亚1609年发表的《莎士比亚十四行诗集》是他最后一部出版的非戏剧类著作，大约成书于1590年至1598年之间，其诗作的结构技巧和语言技巧都很高，几乎每首诗都有独特的审美价值。

《莎士比亚十四行诗集》分为两部分，第一部分为前126首，献给一个年轻的贵族（Fair Lord），诗人的诗热烈歌颂这位朋友的美貌以及他们的友情；第二部分为第127首至最后，献给一位"黑女士"（Dark Lady），描写爱情。

十四行诗是源于意大利民间的一种抒情短诗，文艺复兴初期时盛行于整个欧洲，其结构十分严谨，分为上下两部分，上段为八行，下段为六行，每行十一个音节，韵脚排列为：abba abba，cdc ded。莎士比亚的十四行诗的结构更严谨，他将十四个诗行分为两部分，第一部分为三个四行，第二部分为两行，每行十个音节，韵脚为：abab，cdcd，efef，gg。这样的格式后来被称为"莎士比亚式"或"伊丽莎白式"。对一般诗人而言，诗的结构越严谨就越难抒情，而莎士比亚的十四行诗却毫不拘谨，自由奔放，正如他天马行空的剧作，其诗歌的语言也富于想象，感情充沛。

有一座花园在她的脸上

托马斯·坎皮恩 著

导读:

托马斯·坎皮恩（Thomas Campion，1567—1620）生活在文坛鼎盛、文化活跃的文艺复兴时期，他是纯粹艺术的化身，集诗人、作曲家、文学和音乐理论家为一身。虽然在一段时期被人们所遗忘，但是他对英国文学的贡献无可否认。他的《有一座花园在她的脸上》(*There Is a Garden in Her Face*)以樱桃为主要意象贯穿全诗，描述一个貌美如花且性格刚强的少女。该诗共三节，每节均为ababcc的韵脚，且三节中最后一行诗句的内容一模一样，使得诗歌不但韵味十足，而且主题鲜明。

There Is a Garden in Her Face

There is a garden in her face
Where roses and white lilies grow;
A heav'nly paradise is that place,
Wherein all pleasant fruits do flow;
There cherries grow which none may buy,
Till "Cherry ripe" themselves do cry.

Those cherries fairly do enclose
Of orient pearl a double row,
Which when her lovely laughter shows,
They look like rose-buds filled with snow:
Yet them nor peer nor prince can buy,
Till "Cherry ripe" themselves do cry.

Her eyes like angels watch them still;
Her brows like bended bows do stand,
Threatening with piercing frowns to kill
All that attempt with eye or hand
Those sacred cherries to come nigh,
Till "Cherry ripe" themselves do cry!

有一座花园在她的脸上，①
园内盛开白百合与玫瑰；
那儿是一座庄严的天堂，
还有宜人鲜味累累硕果；
却没人肯把那的樱桃买，②
直到樱桃熟了自己叫卖。

那些樱桃粒粒晶莹浑圆，
犹如双排璀璨珍珠亮洁，③
当她绽开那可爱的笑颜，
就像玫瑰花蕾挂满冰雪：④
可贵族王侯不把樱桃买，
直到樱桃熟了自己叫卖。

她天使般双眼直护樱桃，
她弯弓般双眉竖立守责，
她穿心般双眉发出警告：
欲杀蹑手蹑脚的靠近者，
谁还敢往圣樱桃身边挨，
直到樱桃熟了自己叫卖！

31

注释：

①花园（garden）：用"花园"来比喻俊秀姑娘的面容，暗示出她的美丽和圣洁，这也是歌颂人的美丽和伟大。"花园"的意象使人想到《创世纪》中的伊甸园，以及《雅歌》中的"花园"。参见《雅歌》（4:12）："A garden inclosed is my sister, my spouse,"我的妹子，我的新妇，乃是关锁的园。斯宾塞在《爱情小诗》第64首中也曾写过："Coming to kiss her lips—such grace I found—/Me seemed I smelled a garden of sweet flowers."/我去吻她的唇——我得到这样的恩赐——/我仿佛闻到了满园的花香。

②樱桃（cherries）：指双唇。

③双排璀璨珍珠（Of orient pearl a double row 即 a double row of orient pearl,）：指皓齿。orient原意是东方，此处意为"璀璨夺目的"。

④玫瑰花蕾（rose-buds）：此处指满含皓齿的红唇。

鉴赏：

坎皮恩诗的最大特点，在于它巧妙结合了深思熟虑的精密和合乎传统的质朴。他的诗还具有一定的戏剧性，这一点也很值得关注。他曾是彼特拉克式诗人菲利普·锡德尼的忠实追随者，锡德尼诗语气多变的特点在坎皮恩的诗中皆有体现，这些语气的变化对表达诗人的思想起到了不可磨灭的作用。

坎皮恩精通音乐，因此他的诗具有无与伦比的音乐性。其诗形式极富不规则的变化，而变化中无不流露出诗人的情感趋向。他特别注重每一诗行内以及不同诗行之间的声音效果，这使他的诗具有唯美的声音结构。此外，他爱情诗中的女性形象值得关注，其多首诗都表达对女性尊严的敬重，体现文艺复兴时期以人为本、注重女性的思想。

Psalm 23

The LORD is my shepherd,

I shall not be in want.

He makes me lie down in green pastures:

He leads me beside quiet waters,

He restores my soul.

He guides me in paths of righteousness for his name's sake.

Yea, though I walk through the valley of the shadow of death,

I will fear no evil,

for you are with me;

your rod and your staff,

they comfort me.

You prepare a table before me

in the presence of my enemies:

thou anoint my head with oil;

my cup runneth over.

Surely goodness and love will follow me

all the days of my life:

and I will dwell in the house of the LORD forever.

圣主是我牧羊人，
确实我乃无所求。
他让我卧青草场，
并领我到静水旁，
使我灵魂复原貌，
刻意引我上正道。
虽我穿行死幽谷，
可有你我无所惧。
你之牧杖与短棒，
让我宽慰心舒畅。
每当我敌一出现，
你就为我摆筵席；
在我头上涂膏油，
使我杯酒溢流淌。
在我一生年月日，
幸福关爱定相随：
我将住在圣主堂，
长长久久圣爱享。

鉴赏：

　　《圣咏集》可算是一部诗歌的合集，是旧约的七卷训诲书之一。《圣咏集》堪称历史上最优美的祈祷《诗歌》；选民在各个世代、各次境遇、各种情况中，深切体验、认识、了解到他们与上主之间所有的关系，于是就以祈祷诗的形式把内心的感受充分表达出来，热诚虔敬地向伟大的上主回应。《圣咏集》所收的祈祷诗，全部都产生自选民丰富的生活经验和诚挚的信仰体验，所以，诗歌抒情真切，意义隽永。

离别赠言：莫伤悲

约翰·多恩 著

导读：

　　作为玄学派大师，英国诗人约翰·多恩（John Donne，1572—1631）走的是一条以比喻传达思想，通过思想表达感情的新路。《离别赠言：莫悲伤》（*A Valediction: Forbidding Mourning*）是1611年作者随罗伯特·特鲁里爵士出使巴黎时，在临行前赠给妻子的诗。在这首诗中，诗人把夫妻关系喻为圆规两只脚的关系。妻子是定脚，稳立中心，当丈夫离别（即一只脚移动）时，妻子（定脚）也随之转动，喻夫妻虽然分离，却彼此相连，互相支撑。只有妻子（定脚）坚定地稳立中心，才能使圆圈画得完美，暗示爱人的忠贞不渝才能使他一生美满。该诗赞颂恋人之间更深层次的精神之爱，这种爱不因分离而受到破坏。

A Valediction: Forbidding Mourning

As virtuous men pass mildly away,
    And whisper to their souls to go,
Whilst some of their sad friends do say,
    The breath goes now, and some say, No:

So let us melt, and make no noise,
    No tear-floods nor sigh-tempests move;
'Twere profanation of our joys
    To tell the laity our love.

Moving of th' earth brings harms and fears;
    Men reckon what it did and meant;
But trepidation of the spheres,
    Though greater far, is innocent.

Dull sublunary lovers' love
    (Whose soul is sense) cannot admit
Absence, because it doth remove
    Those things which elemented it.

正如善良者安详离世，
　　轻声向自己灵魂辞别，
有悲伤友人说其断气，
　　而有些却有不同评价。

让我们消停下莫吵了，
　　莫泪水如潮叹声如暴；
那是亵渎我们的快乐——
　　我们的爱与俗人相告。

地动带来伤害与惧怕，
　　人们猜其行且断其意；
对天体的恐惧虽更大，
　　可这恐惧却尤显无知。

无聊的世俗恋人之爱
　　（心灵是感觉）无法
接受分离是因一分开，
　　爱的根基就无处可扎。

But we, by a love so much refined

    That we our selves know not what it is,

Inter-assured of the mind,

    Care less, eyes, lips and hands to miss.

Our two souls, therefore, which are one,

    Though I must go, endure not yet

A breach, but an expansion,

    Like gold to airy thinness beat.

If they be two, they are two so

    As stiff twin compasses are two;

Thy soul the fixed foot, makes no show

    To move, but doth, if the other do.

And though it in the center sit,

    Yet when the other far doth roam,

It leans and harkens after it,

    And grows erect, as that comes home.

Such wilt thou be to me, who must,

    Like th' other foot, obliquely run;

Thy firmness makes my circle just,

    And makes me end where I begun.

可我们的爱优雅绝伦,
　　那是什么我们不知晓,
在乎内心的相互信任,
　　错过视觉触觉不在乎。

两个灵魂故合二为一,
　　虽然我必须离乡背井,
情思不变却得以延续,
　　像镀上薄薄金子一层。

若说两恋人各自一体,
　　那么他们像直脚圆规;
你的心为脚固定不移,
　　另一只脚却移动相随。

一只脚虽然坐定中心,
　　可另一只脚在外游离,
前脚便会倾听而侧身,
　　后脚回家时挺直了腰。

既然你我的关系如此,
　　我得像后脚一样斜跑,
你的坚定使我心中有底,
　　让圆在起点画上句号。

埃里克·吉尔

《Clare》

《神圣十四行诗》第10首

约翰·多恩 著

导读：

  约翰·多恩在自己的诗歌中常常与他人争辩，因此，他在不少诗中常采用辩论的语气，《神圣十四行诗》（*Holy Sonnets*）第10首即以这种方式写成。本诗发表于1633年，是多恩19首《神圣十四行诗》中的第10首。在这首诗中，诗人将敏捷的思维和激情融为一体，在斥责死亡时采用其特有的辩论口吻。本诗没有繁辞丽藻，只有口语化、戏剧化的思辨，显得刚健有力。

Holy Sonnet X

Death, be not proud, though some have called thee
Mighty and dreadful, for, thou art not so,
For, those, whom thou think'st, thou dost overthrow,
Die not, poor Death, nor yet canst thou kill me;
From rest and sleep, which but thy pictures be,
Much pleasure, then from thee, much more must flow,
And soonest our best men with thee do go,
Rest of their bones, and soul's delivery.
Thou art slave to fate, chance, kings, and desperate men,
And dost with poison, war, and sickness dwell,
And poppy, or charms can make us sleep as well,
And better than thy stroke; why swell'st thou then?
One short sleep past, we wake eternally,
And death shall be no more; Death, thou shalt die.

死神，你别骄傲，尽管有人说：
你强大而可怕，可你名不符实；
你以为已把芸芸众生统统杀死，
却不然，可怜死神并未杀死我。
休憩和睡眠不过只是你的写照，
你肯定比休眠更让人感到惬意，
而我们最出色者越早随你而去，
肉体越早安息，灵魂越有寄托。
你是时运、君主和狂徒的从属，
与毒药、战争和病魔勾搭成奸，
罂粟或者符咒也能让我们安眠，
其效果更佳，你何必用心良苦？
我们小憩后，精神将永远清醒，
而再也不死，死神你必将失败。

鉴赏：

多恩的诗歌处处体现离经叛道的思想：其爱情观不落俗套，强调精神与肉体的结合才是真爱；在其宗教诗中，没有对上帝的顶礼膜拜，却有对原罪与救赎、死亡与复活的理性思考。身处动荡不安的时代，多恩没有全盘接收或否认新的科学发现，而是选择性地完成对新宇宙观的吸收与对旧宇宙观的改造。新颖别致的内容呼唤着与之相匹配的表现形式。多恩在诗中大胆地采用貌似毫无关联的奇喻、充满矛盾的悖论以及富有戏剧性的口语体，从而实现感情的哲理化、思维的理性化。多恩的诗以其不落俗套的内容和新颖别致的形式实现理性与感性的完美结合，启迪和影响了以 T.S 艾略特为代表的一大批现代主义诗人。

评论家们对玄学派诗歌的研究取得以下共识：玄学派诗歌多有新颖独特的意象，多醉心于客观与微观世界中的奇想，节奏和韵律多变，且有复杂的主题（宗教的和世俗的），展现出对似是而非论点的喜好，并常有直截了当的表达方式，对传统道德观念的质疑等等。1986年在美国正式成立多恩研究会，充分表明以多恩为代表的玄学派诗歌在英美文学发展史上的重要地位。

献给西莉亚的歌（上）

本·琼生 著

导读：

　　"及时行乐"，作为文学中的一种主题以及文学作品中所表现的一种思想，在其发展和演变过程中与欧洲以及世界各个历史时期的思潮有着密不可分的关联。有人认为，"及时行乐"的内涵并非一般意义上的消极处世，而是积极人生的反映，它甚至超出文学的范围，在人类思想史上的人学与神学、现世主义与来世主义，以及封建意识与人文主义思想的冲突中发挥应有的作用。"及时行乐"的世界观影响了17世纪古典主义作家本·琼生（Ben Jonson，1572—1637）等诗人。本·琼生不仅对这一世界观极力称赞，而且还将其反映在自己的《献给西莉亚的歌（上）》[*Song: To Celia*（Ⅰ）]这首诗作中。

Song: To Celia (I)

Come, my Celia, let us prove,
While we can, the sports of love;
Time will not be ours forever,
He at length our good will sever;
Spend not then his gifts in vain,
Suns that set may rise again;
But if once we lose this light,
'Tis with us perpetual night.
Why should we defer our joys?
Fame and rumour are but toys.
Cannot we delude the eyes
Of a few poor household spies?
Or his easier ears beguile,
Thus removed by our wile?
'Tis no sin love's fruits to steal;
But the sweet theft to reveal,
To be taken, to be seen,
Those have crimes accounted been.

来吧，西莉亚！趁年轻，
让我们来求证爱的路径；
光阴并不总归我们所有，
它终将断送美好的愿求；
切莫徒劳耗费时光馈赠，
夕阳西下总会再现日出；
可是一旦我们失去阳光，
伴我们的将是黑夜漫长。
为何要把欢乐时光推迟？
名声和谣言不过是玩物。
我们能骗过谁的千里眼，
骗过些可怜的家庭侦探？
还能骗过他们的顺风耳，
我们的计谋能把耳堵塞？
偷取爱情果实并非犯罪；
可举报爱情的窃贼行为，
无论被抓捕还是被看到，
都已算得上是罪责难逃。

爱德华·蒙克

《清晨》

献给西莉亚的歌（下）

本·琼生 著

导读：

《献给西莉亚之歌（下）》[*Song: To Celia* (II)]是本·琼生另一首通俗易懂、幽默诙谐的抒情短诗。由于该诗音韵悠扬，曾被谱成曲，颇受男女青年青睐，因而广为流传。在这首诗中，诗人把爱情提到极高的位置，他在灵魂深处一直渴望爱神的降临，一旦遇到钟情的人，就祈求她只需用眼睛看着他，与他对饮，或在酒杯口上留下吻痕，哪怕天上降下玉露琼浆，也不愿用美酒换取她的眼神。该诗虽未描写西莉亚的容貌，可她的美貌气质却隐隐约约浮现在字里行间，这是该诗写作技巧所在。诗歌分为两段，韵脚是abcb，abcb；defe，defe。

Song: To Celia (II)

Drink to me only with thine eyes,
And I will pledge with mine;
Or leave a kiss but in the cup,
And I'll not look for wine.
The thirst that from the soul doth rise
Doth ask a drink divine;
But might I of Jove's nectar sup,
I would not change for thine.

I sent thee late a rosy wreath,
Not so much honouring thee
As giving it a hope that there
It could not withered be.
But thou thereon didst only breathe,
And sent'st it back to me;
Since when it grows and smells, I swear,
Not of itself but thee!

你只需用眼神与我干杯，
我定发誓用目光回应您。
或将你的吻留在杯口上，
我就不必寻觅佳酿饮品。
这种渴望发自我的心扉，
唯有祈求一杯圣酒暖心。
纵使我喝下酒神的琼浆，
也不愿用它换你的眼神。

我刚送你一顶玫瑰花冠，
并不只为攀爬你的高枝，
却只为献上玫瑰以期盼，
让玫瑰花今后永不凋敝。
然而你闻过玫瑰的花瓣，
之后将玫瑰送还我自己；
从此玫瑰绽放香气弥漫，
我敢说只因你花香飘溢！

鉴赏：

本·琼生作为"桂冠诗人"和英国古典文学的先驱，是继莎士比亚之后重要的英国文学家，是詹姆士一世生前最喜爱的剧作家之一。其诗作节制、典雅，讲究音律，语言明快、优美，常用宁静、富有韵律的传统意象。

抒情诗《献给西莉亚的歌》是琼生爱情诗歌的代表作。该诗立意清新、意境融洽、韵律优美，联想丰富，淋漓尽致地刻画一位陷入单恋的男子如痴如醉的形象，并高度赞美和歌颂柏拉图式的爱情，即纯洁的精神恋爱。全诗的结构、用词、节奏和音韵安排合理，诗人以其独特的方式增添和强化这首抒情诗的意境美。诗人主要运用味觉、嗅觉和视觉意象表达对爱情的歌颂和向往。《献给西莉亚的歌》写的是精神之恋，其中情感的表达不是通过肢体的接触，而是成功运用朴实无华的语言，丰富的意象和大胆的想象，达到情景交融的优美意境，能够给人以强烈的美感。

致少女：珍惜时光

罗伯特·赫里克 著

导读：

《致少女：珍惜时光》(*To the Virgins, to Make Much of Time*)是英国资产阶级时期和复辟时期所谓"骑士派"诗人之一的罗伯特·赫里克（Robert Herrick，1591—1674）的抒情诗代表作之一，其主题是"及时行乐"。该诗首节起句中的"玫瑰花蕾"极富意蕴；在第二节，诗人把目光从世间移向天空，把太阳比作"天灯"；在第三节，诗人笔锋转向人类，从少女的青春活力写到女性的风烛残年。前三节通过意象揭示"天、地、人"之间的关系，很自然引向最后一节"及时行乐"的主题。诗人劝说美丽少女莫错良机，尽享欢乐。

To the Virgins, to Make Much of Time

Gather ye rosebuds while ye may,
    Old Time is still a-flying:
And this same flower that smiles to-day
    To-morrow will be dying.

The glorious lamp of heaven, the sun,
    The higher he's a-getting,
The sooner will his race be run,
    And nearer he's to setting.

That age is best which is the first,
    When youth and blood are warmer;
But being spent, the worse, and worst
    Times still succeed the former.

Then be not coy, but use your time,
    And while ye may, go marry:
For having lost but once your prime,
    You may for ever tarry.

玫蕾堪折直须折，
　　　光阴依旧逝；
今朝此花好颜色，
　　　翌日将凋敝。

灼灼彤日若天灯，
　　　渐往高处至；
渐行渐快其行程，
　　　渐近黄昏时。

豆蔻年华妙龄佳，
　　　青春更热血；
韶华殆尽每况下，
　　　残年风烛灭。

珍惜光阴莫彷徨，
　　　趁早做人妻；
一旦错过好时光，
　　　汝将永蹉跎。

鉴赏：

赫里克是英国资产阶级革命时期和复辟时期的所谓"骑士派"诗人之一。"骑士派"诗主要写宫廷中的调情作乐和好战骑士为君杀敌的荣誉感，宣扬及时行乐。不过赫里克也写有不少清新的田园抒情诗和爱情诗，如《樱桃熟了》《快摘玫瑰花苞》《致水仙》《疯姑娘之歌》等，成为英国诗歌中的名作而永久流传。他的许多诗被谱曲传唱。赫里克传世的约1400首诗分别收在《雅歌》和《西方乐土》中。

赫里克的许多诗作所关心的都是珍惜光阴的话题。他一生写下不少以淳朴的农村生活为题材的抒情诗，以田园抒情诗和爱情抒情诗著称。他的诗集《西方乐土》长久以来一直为人所推崇，原因就在于诗中所体现的抒情风格。

美德

乔治·赫伯特 著

导读：

《美德》(*Virtue*)是 17 世纪玄学派诗人乔治·赫伯特(George Herbert, 1593—1633)的一首短小精悍却极富哲理的佳作。该诗以其简洁生动的语言和丰富的修辞手法感召世人，诗人在诗中所使用的拟人、明喻、暗喻、通感等修辞手法与诗的意境巧妙结合，形成该诗的独特艺术魅力。

Virtue

Sweet day, so cool, so calm, so bright,
   The bridal of the earth and sky;
The dew shall weep thy fall tonight,
     For thou must die.

Sweet rose, whose hue, angry and brave,
   Bids the rash gazer wipe his eyes;
Thy root is ever in its grave,
     And thou must die.

Sweet spring, full of sweet days and roses,
   A box where sweets compacted lie;
My music shows ye have your closes,
     And all must die.

Only a sweet and virtuous soul,
   Like seasoned timber, never gives;
But though the whole world turn to coal.
     Then chiefly lives.

甜蜜的一天，多么凉爽、明亮、静谧，
　　你是天造地设的红娘；
今晚露珠将为你的寂灭哭泣，
　　　因你注定消亡。

芬芳的玫瑰，尽情怒放、色彩艳丽，
　　你请性急观众拭目凝望；
可是你的根须总是扎在墓地，
　　　而你注定消亡。

甜蜜的春天，日日甜蜜、玫香四溢，
　　你是一只花匣，匣里留有余香；
我的音乐表明你有凋零的一日，
　　　而万物注定消亡。

只有美好而高尚的灵魂，
　　才会像风干木材永不变样；
尽管整个世界化为灰烬，
　　　可它依旧留存。

The Invocation from Paradise Lost

Of Man's first disobedience, and the fruit
Of that forbidden tree, whose mortal taste
Brought death into the world, and all our woe,
With loss of Eden, till one greater Man
Restore us, and regain the blissful seat,
Sing, Heavenly Muse, that on the secret top
Of Oreb, or of Sinai, didst inspire
That Shepherd who first taught the chosen seed,
In the beginning how the heavens and earth
Rose out of Chaos: or, if Sion Hill
Delight thee more, and Siloa's brook that flowed
Fast by the oracle of God, I thence
Invoke thy aid to my adventrous song,
That with no middle flight intends to soar
Above th' Aonian Mount, while it pursues
Things unattempted yet in prose or rhyme.
And chiefly thou, O Spirit, that dost prefer
Before all temples th' upright heart and pure,
Instruct me, for thou know'st; Thou from the first
Wast present, and with mighty wings outspread,

人类最初忤逆天命偷尝禁果，
把死亡和所有苦痛带至人间，
于是我们就失去了伊甸乐园，
直到出现一个更伟大的人物，
为我们恢复并重获这片乐土。
天国的缪斯女神站在何烈山
或西奈山神峰启迪那牧羊人，
向第一个选民宣讲太初年代
天地是如何在混沌之中生成；
或者锡安山是否更使你高兴，
或者西罗亚的小溪是否按照
上帝的神谕湍急地向前流动。
在那儿求你助我写冒险之歌，
达到平庸者不敢逾越的高度，
越过爱奥尼峰后让我去追逐
在诗歌或散文中未尝的东西。
关键时刻您是我精神力量啊，
在所有神庙前更悉心指引我。
因为你知道一开始你就在此，
展开你那副强大有力的翅膀，

Dove-like sat'st brooding on the vast abyss,
And mad'st it pregnant: what in me is dark
Illumine; what is low raise and support;
That to the height of this great argument,
I may assert Eternal Providence,
And justify the ways of God to men.

如鸽子一般坐在巨大深渊上,
沉思如何照亮我内心的黑暗;
提升并且支撑我卑微的心理;
水平达到这场大辩论的高度,
我就能阐明永恒不朽的天意,
而且证明上帝你的为人之道。

鉴赏：

　　《失乐园》表现出人的奋争和救赎，既是触及人类心灵的作品，也是对人类最深层的道德、精神和信仰的探索，折射出弥尔顿对人和人性、对人类不幸根源和人类如何才能得到拯救等议题的思考。救赎主题具体体现在长诗题材的选取和人物形象的塑造上。弥尔顿《失乐园》在题材选取上借人类始祖亚当、夏娃受撒旦引诱堕落而被逐出乐园的故事，揭示基督教"原罪"观念，提倡人类应以现实的态度勇于承担尘世生活的重担，以赎罪拯救自身。《失乐园》出于表达救赎这一崇高思想的需要，以宏大的事件为题材，以宏伟的长诗为体裁，并以引经据典、气势恢宏的风格，创造了文学史上经典的人物形象。在人物形象塑造上带有诗人救赎思想的烙印：其中亚当和夏娃身上所具有人类普遍的品质是救赎的条件；耶稣是诗人理想人格的化身；美德是救赎的基础；堕落与再生给人类带来救赎的希望。

致我亲爱的丈夫

安妮·布拉德斯特里特 著

导读：

《致我亲爱的丈夫》(*To My Dear and Loving Husband*)是美国女诗人安妮·布拉德斯特里特（Anne Bradstreet，1612—1672）的一首诗，从一个侧面反映北美清教徒的生活。诗人生活的年代，新英格兰初建神权统治，清教主义盛行。作为一位总督的女儿、另一位总督的妻子，诗人在其情感世界中显得拘谨古板，缺少自然成分。然而，诗人在这首诗中完全超越宗教信仰和清规戒律，像一只出笼的小鸟在无际的天空自由翱翔。

To My Dear and Loving Husband

If ever two were one, then surely we;
If ever man were loved by wife, then thee;
If ever wife was happy in a man,
Compare with me, ye women, if you can.
I prize thy love more than whole mines of gold,
Or all the riches that the East doth hold.
My love is such that rivers cannot quench,
Nor ought but love from thee, give recompense.
Thy love is such I can no way repay;
The heavens reward thee manifold, I pray.
Then while we live, in love let's so persever,
That when we live no more, we may live ever.

若有并蒂莲，那我们定相挨；
若有妻爱夫，那定是你被爱；
若有妻子陶醉在丈夫怀抱里，
那么女人中又有谁能跟我比。
我得到你的爱胜过整座金山，
胜过东印度公司所有之财产。
我如此的爱焰江水难以扑灭，
我的爱只有你的爱能予酬谢。
你如此地爱我让我无以报偿，
我祈求上天要对你多方奖赏。
在世时让我们如此挚爱一生，
离世时我们的生命方得永恒。

鉴赏：

　　布拉德斯特里特，清教徒诗人，1630年从英国来到新大陆马萨诸塞湾殖民地，以《第十位缪斯在美洲出现》（*The Tenth Muse Lately Sprung up in America*, 1650）闻名于世。其中大部分诗都是冗长的模仿性作品，只有最后两首《凡人的虚荣》（*Of the Vanity of All Worldly Creatures*）和《大卫对扫罗和约拿单的哀悼》（*David's Lamentation for Sauland Jonathan*）独具风格，意境纯真。

　　她后来的一些诗歌是为她的家庭而写，表现她全心接受清教徒教义以后在精神上的成长过程。《灵与肉》（*The Flesh and the Spirit*），因为没有说教而受人喜爱。她也写过一些动人的和更富有个人色彩的诗，其中《献给我亲爱的丈夫》（*To My Dear and Loving Husband*）、《人世正凋萎，万物有终极》（*All Things within This Fading World hath End*）描写她在生孩子之前的思想；《心痛手颤写诗句》（*With Troubled Heart and Trembling Hand I Write*）写一个孙儿之死。

致羞怯的情人

安德鲁·马维尔 著

导读：

《致羞怯的情人》（*To His Coy Mistress*）是英国17世纪著名诗人安德鲁·马维尔（Andrew Marvell，1621—1678）的一首代表诗作。该首诗结构严谨，构思奇妙，意象独特，音韵优美，文笔流畅。艾略特在评论他的诗时说："马维尔能将炙热的感情、敏锐的理智表现出典雅的抒情格调。"此外，该诗之所以能从众多同类主题的诗歌中脱颖而出，在英国文学史占有一席之地，成为英美大学生教科书中脍炙人口的不朽诗篇，主要是因为诗人在诗中使用逻辑推理的说理方式，让抒情当中多了理性的色彩。

To His Coy Mistress

    Had we but world enough and time,
This coyness, lady, were no crime.
We would sit down, and think which way
To walk, and pass our long love's day.
Thou by the Indian Ganges' side
Shouldst rubies find; I by the tide
Of Humber would complain. I would
Love you ten years before the Flood;
And you should, if you please, refuse
Till the conversion of the Jews.
My vegetable love should grow
Vaster than empires, and more slow.
An hundred years should go to praise
Thine eyes, and on thy forehead gaze;
Two hundred to adore each breast;
But thirty thousand to the rest;
An age at least to every part,
And the last age should show your heart.
For, lady, you deserve this state;
Nor would I love at lower rate.
    But at my back I always hear

我们只要有足够的时空,
姑娘哟,羞怯不当罪控。
可坐下思考散步的道路,
将漫长的爱情时光共度。
你身处印度国恒河之滨,
应该还在将红宝石寻遍,
可我在亨伯河倾诉衷肠,
洪荒前十年我把你爱上。
你可随己心意将我拒绝,
直至犹太人与信仰决裂。
我满腔的爱意与日俱增,
该缓缓溢满整个帝国城。
我一生赞美你深情双眼,
我的双眸注视你的额前;
来生还赞美你心中柔情;
爱你三万年直到呼吸停;
你至少从生到死的每日,
天天都应表白你的心迹。
姑娘哟,因你配得起爱;
我对你的爱从不敢懈怠。
但我常听见在我的身后,

Time's winged chariot hurrying near;
And yonder all before us lie
Deserts of vast eternity.
Thy beauty shall no more be found.
Nor, in thy marble vault, shall sound
My echoing song.Then worms shall try
That long preserved virginity;
And your quaint honour turn to dust;
And into ashes all my lust.
The grave's a fine and private place,
But none, I think, do there embrace.

   Now, therefore, while the youthful hue
Sits on thy skin like morning dew,
And while thy willing soul transpires
At every pore with instant fires.
Now let us sport us while we may;
And now, like amorous birds of prey,
Rather at once our time devour
Than languish in his slow-chapped power.
Let us roll all our strength and all
Our sweetness up into one ball;
And tear our pleasures with rough strife
Through the iron gates of life:
Thus, though we cannot make our sun
Stand still, yet we will make him run.

岁月的飞轮正朝我凑近。
我们的眼前有一片土地，
那是茫茫荒野一望无际。
在你那大理石的墓穴下，
我寻君美貌而别无他法；
你却听不到回荡的歌声，
虫蛆将品尝你久藏童贞。
你玉洁的坚贞变为灰尘，
我满腔的情欲化作灰烬。
坟墓是幽静沉寂的地方，
可谁也不会在那里相拥。

  因而现在趁你青春容颜
好像朝露在皮肤上驻足，
你心甘情愿在每个毛孔
将顷刻燃烧的火焰喷涌；
让我们像笼中的爱情鸟，
趁早寻欢作乐莫错良宵！
宁可在即兴欢乐中度过，
也都胜过在苦思中蹉跎。
让一切的活力滚成球体，
将所有的甜蜜融为一体！
我们顽强冲破生活铁门，
去赢得我们应有的欢欣。
即使难让太阳静止不动，
我们也能伴着太阳飞奔！

鉴赏：

马维尔是17世纪英国著名的玄学派诗人。玄学派诗歌的突出特征在于对新颖的意象和奇特比喻的运用。玄学派诗歌语言口语化，节奏和韵律有很大灵活性，主题复杂，充满智慧与创造力。马维尔与其他玄学派诗人不同，被一些批评家看作是承前启后的诗人。他不但继承伊丽莎白时代爱情诗中的浪漫主义传统，成为一位具有浪漫主义气质的诗人，而且开启18世纪古典主义的"理性时代"。浪漫派诗人偏重情感的自然流露；古典派诗人则偏重意象的完整优美，喜以哲理入诗。作为玄学派诗人，马维尔体现出许多玄学派诗人突出的特征，即善于用奇特的意象和别致的比喻，比如《致羞怯的情人》用了"笼中的爱情鸟""让一切的活力滚成球体""生活铁门""伴着太阳飞奔"等奇思妙喻。

我是生存的面包
——沉思录之八

爱德华·泰勒 著

导读：

  爱德华·泰勒（Edward Taylor，1642—1729），是在英国出生的美国清教派牧师和诗人，殖民时期备受清教徒推崇的两个重要的宗教诗人之一，美国文学拓荒时期宗教诗歌具有代表性的诗人，被公认为是美国19世纪前最重要的诗人，他在有生之年仅发表过两首诗歌。直到1937年，人们在研究他的手稿时才认识到他那虔诚的诗歌的优美绝伦。他以独树一帜的诗歌形式探索基督教的教义和教徒所信奉的"原始罪恶"。《我是生存的面包——沉思录之八》（*I Am the Living Bread: Meditation 8*）主要表达这样的宗教思想：人人都注定要受到永恒的惩罚，换取来世幸福的唯一办法是今世苦行。该诗堪称17世纪美国诗坛的佳作。

I Am the Living Bread: Meditation 8

I kenning through Astronomy Divine
    The World's bright Battlement, wherein I spy
A Golden Path my pencil cannot line,
    From that bright Throne unto my Threshold lie.
    And while my puzzled thoughts about it pore
    I find the Bread of Life in't at my door.

When that this Bird of Paradise put in
    This Wicker Cage (my Corpse) to tweedle praise
Had pecked the Fruit forbade: and so did fling
    Away its Food; and lost its golden days;
    It fell into Celestial Famine sore:
    And never could attain a morsel more.

Alas! Alas! Poore Bird, what wilt thou do?
    The Creatures' field no food for Souls e'er gave.
And if thou knock at Angels' doors they show
    An Empty Barrel: they no soul bread have.
    Alas! Poor Bird, the World's White Loaf is done.
    And cannot yield thee here the smallest Crumb.

透过神圣的天文望远镜我正看见
　　人间明亮城墙，置身其间我细看，
看出铅笔难勾画的金光大道出现，
　　它从明亮的宝座延伸至我的门槛。
　　而我对此迷惑不解地把思绪寻找，
　　我看见门槛上有一块生存的面包。

当天堂的这只小鸟飞进这把鸟笼，
　　在鸟笼（我的尸）里鸟儿颂歌啼，
吃了粒禁果后：展开翅膀飞匆匆，
　　衔走它的食物却错过它的黄金日；
　　鸟儿陷入天上的饥荒而深感痛处：
　　再也无法获得多那么一点的谷物。

哎呀！哎呀！可怜鸟儿你能做啥？
　　动物不种粮，因为食物只供给生灵。
你若敲天使之门，他们只让你看到
　　那是只空桶：他们没把人间面包备。
　　哎呀！可怜鸟儿，人间白面已出炉。
　　而你在此却做不出小小的白面馍。

In this sad state, God's Tender Bowels run
    Out streams of Grace: And He to end all strife
The Purest Wheat in Heaven His dear-dear son
    Grinds, and kneads up into this Bread of Life.
    Which bread of life from Heaven Down came and stands
    Dished on thy Table up by Angels' Hands.

Did God mold up this Bread in Heaven, and bake,
    Which from His Table came, and to thine goeth?
Doth He bespeak thee thus, This Soul Bread take.
    Come Eat thy fill of this thy God's White Loaf?
    Its Food too fine for angels, yet come, take
    And Eat thy fill. Its heavens sugar cake.

What Grace is this knead in this Loaf? This thing
    Souls are but petty things it to admire.
Ye Angels, help: This fill would to the brim
    Heav'ns whelmed-down crystal meal bowl, yea and higher
    This bread of life dropped in thy mouth, doth cry.
    Eat, Eat me, Soul, and thou shalt never die.

可在此惨状下，从上帝温暖心田
　　冒出恩惠的蒸气：平息一切纷争。
天堂最纯的小麦由他儿子亲手碾，
　　揉完面团做成生命的面包也是他，
　　这块生命的面包从神圣天堂下来，
　　并由天使亲自把盘子往你桌上摆。

上帝制作面包，并在天堂里烘烤，
　　面包来自他的桌上，而后献给你。
这样他一定会说：来吃人间面包。
　　来把您上帝做的这块白白面包吃？
　　这食物对天使实在好，可来吃吧，
　　吃您做的面包。这是天堂的甜点。

这块面包含您的什么恩惠？我们
　　这些人都不过是赞美您的小人物。
您的天使来帮忙，这面包大得很，
　　装满天堂闪光之碗，碗中高高竖。
　　生存面包喂入您口，理当叫声好。
　　吃吧，把我吃了吧！您将永不老。

鉴赏：

  泰勒被称为是一位"旷野巴罗克"诗人。他的诗歌闪烁着宗教思想和艺术光芒。他模仿邓恩等英国文艺复兴时期玄学派宗教诗人，将神学思想深藏于日常话语中，用奇喻、双关、悖论等修辞手法，让诗篇充满喜乐与惊奇。《沉思集》是泰勒的代表性诗歌作品，诗人将貌似简单的旷野意象与严肃深邃的宗教主题相互融合，体现出独特的"旷野巴罗克"诗歌创作风格。

  《我是生存的面包——沉思录之八》是泰勒常被选入国内外美国文学选集的最具代表性的一首宗教诗歌。诗的主题是赞美神爱世人，但是他并没有在诗歌开篇时就将主题和盘托出，而是像邓恩等玄学派诗人一样，通过奇思妙想，运用天文隐喻和天体意象，将上帝的形象陌生化，让人觉得上帝并非触手可及。在他看来，不论是神学理论中神圣的天文学，还是诗歌创作中的奇思妙喻，似乎都无法拉近上帝与世人之间的距离。

墓园挽歌

托马斯·格雷 著

导读：

《墓园挽歌》(*Elegy Written in a Country Churchyard*)是英国18世纪重要诗人托马斯·格雷（Thomas Gray，1716—1771）的代表作，他一生虽只写过十来首诗，但却为18世纪的英国，乃至全世界奉献了《墓园挽歌》这样一首著名的诗篇。挽歌有时表达对特殊逝者的悲叹思念，有时表达对某种情境的悲伤感受。格雷的《墓园挽歌》最初提笔于1742年，原本是为哀悼他亲爱的好友理查德·韦斯特，发表于1751年，其写作初衷是对友人的哀思，可内容的表达却大大超出预期的目的。

Elegy Written in a Country Churchyard

The curfew tolls the knell of parting day,
    The lowing herd winds slowly o'er the lea,
The ploughman homeward plods his weary way,
    And leaves the world to darkness and to me.

Now fades the glimmering landscape on the sight,
    And all the air a solemn stillness holds,
Save where the beetle wheels his droning flight,
    And drowsy tinklings lull the distant folds;

Save that from yonder ivy-mantled tower
    The moping owl does to the moon complain
Of such, as wandering near her secret bower,
    Molest her ancient solitary reign.

Beneath those rugged elms, that yew-tree's shade,
    Where heaves the turf in many a mouldering heap,
Each in his narrow cell for ever laid,
    The rude Forefathers of the hamlet sleep.

晚钟阵阵响音送走白昼,
　草原上羊群迂回声声落,
回家疲惫耕农缓缓行走,
　这世界留给黄昏留给我。

闪烁的风景在眼前渐退,
　一片肃静气息锁住人寰,
只听嗡嗡甲虫绕圈纷飞,
　沉闷铃声静于远处羊栏;

只听在爬满春藤的塔下,
　一只忧郁之枭对月诉苦,
怪人无端闯其秘密之家,
　骚扰其古老僻静的领土。

扁柏遮阴的粗糙榆树下,
　鼓鼓草皮覆盖众烂土堆,
各自一直躺在洞窟旮旯,
　鲁莽的祖先在那儿安睡。

The breezy call of incense-breathing morn,
    The swallow twittering from the straw-built shed,
The cock's shrill clarion, or the echoing horn,
    No more shall rouse them from their lowly bed.

For them no more the blazing hearth shall burn,
    Or busy housewife ply her evening care:
No children run to lisp their sire's return,
    Or climb his knees the envied kiss to share,

Oft did the harvest to their sickle yield,
    Their furrow oft the stubborn glebe has broke;
How jocund did they drive their team afield!
    How bow'd the woods beneath their sturdy stroke!

Let not Ambition mock their useful toil,
    Their homely joys, and destiny obscure;
Nor Grandeur hear with a disdainful smile
    The short and simple annals of the Poor.

The boast of heraldry, the pomp of power,
    And all that beauty, all that wealth e'er gave,
Awaits alike th' inevitable hour.
    The paths of glory lead but to the grave.

飘香的晨风轻快地呼叫，
　　燕子在草窝里啭鸣呢喃，
公鸡的尖叫或号角回声，
　　不再唤醒祖先黄泉长眠。

熊熊炉火不再为其燃烧，
　　忙碌家妇不为夜活较真：
孩子不为父亲归来报告，
　　不爬他膝共享家庭时光，

往常一开镰就丰收在即，
　　硬泥板让他们犁出垄沟；
他们欢快地赶牲口下地，
　　猛砍之下树木棵棵低头！

野心者莫嘲讽他们实干，
　　莫嘲家常乐与无名宿命；
富人们也切莫轻蔑冷眼，
　　莫笑听穷人的简短生平。

门第炫耀以及权贵显赫，
　　一切美貌财富种种好处，
都等待难逃一劫的时刻：
　　荣光之路终将引向坟墓。

Nor you, ye Proud, impute to these the fault
    If Memory o'er their tomb no trophies raise,
Where through the long-drawn aisle and fretted vault
    The pealing anthem swells the note of praise.

Can storied urn or animated bust
    Back to its mansion call the fleeting breath?
Can Honour's voice provoke the silent dust,
    Or Flattery soothe the dull cold ear of Death?

Perhaps in this neglected spot is laid
    Some heart once pregnant with celestial fire;
Hands, that the rod of empire might have sway'd,
    Or waked to ecstasy the living lyre.

But Knowledge to their eyes her ample page,
    Rich with the spoils of time, did ne'er unroll;
Chill Penury repress'd their noble rage,
    And froze the genial current of the soul.

Full many a gem of purest ray serene,
    The dark unfathom'd caves of ocean bear:
Full many a flower is born to blush unseen,
    And waste its sweetness on the desert air.

骄傲者别怪这些人错行，
　　缅怀者没为其建造祭堂，
没让长廊道和雕花拱顶
　　回响洪亮赞歌以表颂扬。

生动雕像以及铭文坟墓，
　　岂能唤醒死人回归家舍？
赞誉岂能激发无言尘土？
　　献媚岂能安慰死神钝耳？

也许这方土地尽是荒芜，
　　某颗心曾怀着天上之火；
双手本可执掌帝王之芴，
　　或神奇地把七弦琴弹拨。

可知识从未为他们翻开
　　那世代累积的连篇书卷；
贫寒压抑其高尚的情怀，
　　冻结其心中友善的清泉。

世上多少晶莹剔透珠宝
　　在深不可测的黑暗海底；
世上多少鲜花谁人见晓，
　　其香白白散在苍凉天际。

Some village-Hampden, that with dauntless breast
    The little tyrant of his fields withstood;
Some mute inglorious Milton here may rest,
    Some Cromwell, guiltless of his country's blood.

Th' applause of list'ning senates to command,
    The threats of pain and ruin to despise,
To scatter plenty o'er a smiling land,
    And read their history in a nation's eyes,

Their lot forbade: nor circumscribed alone
    Their growing virtues, but their crimes confined;
Forbade to wade through slaughter to a throne,
    And shut the gates of mercy on mankind,

The struggling pangs of conscious truth to hide,
    To quench the blushes of ingenuous shame,
Or heap the shrine of Luxury and Pride
    With incense kindled at the Muse's flame.

Far from the madding crowd's ignoble strife,
    Their sober wishes never learn'd to stray;
Along the cool sequester'd vale of life
    They kept the noiseless tenour of their way.

某村民定如汉普登①般勇敢，
　　胆大反抗当地那小恶霸；
在这睡的可会有弥尔顿？
　　亦不会有暴君克伦威尔。

赢得在场元老雷鸣鼓掌，
　　无视威胁全然不顾生死，
用鲜血染红微笑的土壤，
　　在国人眼里读自己历史，

他们的命运不允许这样：
　　以放纵罪过来培养德性；
通过杀戮从而当上国王，
　　对世上众人关仁慈之门；

隐藏起良知的挣扎苦涩，
　　抑制天真羞愧红遍脸上。
不堆筑奢骄的古老神社；
　　不用缪斯火焰点燃熏香。

远离芸芸众生勾心斗角，
　　明确地希望永不用流浪，
沿着生活清凉僻静山坳，
　　坚持走正道而不做声响。

Yet ev'n these bones from insult to protect
   Some frail memorial still erected nigh,
   With uncouth rhymes and shapeless sculpture deck'd,
Implores the passing tribute of a sigh.

Their name, their years, spelt by th' unletter'd Muse,
   The place of fame and elegy supply:
And many a holy text around she strews,
   That teach the rustic moralist to die.

For who, to dumb forgetfulness a prey,
   This pleasing anxious being e'er resign'd,
Left the warm precincts of the cheerful day,
   Nor cast one longing lingering look behind?

On some fond breast the parting soul relies,
   Some pious drops the closing eye requires;
Ev'n from the tomb the voice of Nature cries,
   Ev'n in our ashes live their wonted fires.

For thee, who, mindful of th' unhonour'd dead,
   Dost in these lines their artless tale relate;
If chance, by lonely contemplation led,
   Some kindred spirit shall inquire thy fate,—

即使保护骨头免受侮辱,
　　脆弱的纪念碑附近竖起,
用拙劣韵语和无形雕塑,
　　恳求过往行人道声叹息。

文盲缪斯拼写姓名年份,
　　还拼写地址和一篇悼词;
她在周围撒满神圣经文,
　　教质朴道德家如何谢世。

谁愿做愚蠢猎物而健忘,
　　坦然丢下忧喜参半之身,
谁愿离开那温馨的现场,
　　而不依依不舍顾盼一阵?

离别之灵傍在情之怀抱,
　　临闭双目祈求虔诚之泪,
哪怕发自坟墓自然哭号,
　　哪怕旧火燃于我们的灰。

为你我关注无名的死人,
　　以诗句诉说质朴的故事,
某亲属假若与你有缘分,
　　会在独思中用心问身世,——

97

Haply some hoary-headed swain may say,
    "Oft have we seen him at the peep of dawn
Brushing with hasty steps the dews away,
    To meet the sun upon the upland lawn.

"There at the foot of yonder nodding beech
    That wreathes its old fantastic roots so high,
His listless length at noontide would he stretch,
    And pore upon the brook that babbles by.

"Hard by yon wood, now smiling as in scorn,
    Muttering his wayward fancies he would rove,
Now drooping, woeful wan, like one forlorn,
    Or crazed with care, or cross'd in hopeless love.

"One morn I miss'd him on the custom'd hill,
    Along the heath, and near his favourite tree;
Another came; nor yet beside the rill,
    Nor up the lawn, nor at the wood was he;

"The next with dirges due in sad array
    Slow through the church-way path we saw him borne.
Approach and read (for thou canst read) the lay
    Graved on the stone beneath yon aged thorn."

也许有白发村民对他说,
　我们常看见他天还未亮,
其匆匆脚步把露水扫落,
　上高处草地去迎接朝阳;

在那边婆娑的榉木树头,
　隆起的老根盘错在一起,
他常在那慵懒伸展午休,
　细看身旁那条潺潺小溪。

远处硬木时而笑中讽嘲,
　念念有词发出奇谈怪议,
时而垂头丧气似无依靠,
　或似心忧或似情场失意。

一清早在他常去的山头,
　他未在丛中爱树下出现;
翌日早尽管我走下溪流,
　上草地穿树林他仍不见。

次日我们见到送葬队列,
　慢行过教堂道看他下葬,——
上前看老荆棘下的碑碣,
　你要能念就念这些诗行。

99

The Epitaph

Here rests his head upon the lap of Earth
    A youth to Fortune and to Fame unknown.
Fair Science frowned not on his humble birth,
    And Melancholy marked him for her own.

Large was his bounty, and his soul sincere,
    Heaven did a recompense as largely send:
He gave to Misery all he had, a tear,
    He gained from Heaven ('twas all he wish'd) a friend.

No farther seek his merits to disclose,
    Or draw his frailties from their dread abode,
(There they alike in trembling hope repose),
    The bosom of his Father and his God

挽歌

一青年头枕这地球膝盖，
　　相伴莫名的命运与声誉。
公平科学不鄙卑微何在，
　　忧者因她忧郁将他铭记。

他无比慷慨且真心实意，
　　上天没给予他巨大回报：
他为自己周身不幸哭泣，
　　却在天堂交到一位朋友。

父亲再不找他优点称颂，
　　也不从他短处找其弱点，
（优缺点都安眠于虚幻中），
　　在上帝的那怀抱中安眠。

注释：

　　① 指 John Hampden，反对英王查理斯一世征收造舰税（Ship money），并最终引起了英国内战。——编者注

鉴赏：

《墓园挽歌》是格雷的代表作，其主题是：人不分高低贵贱，最后都要进入坟墓，虽然这是老生常谈，但他提出不但哀悼祖先，而且要哀悼包括自己在内所有的人，这就使诗具有普遍意义。

该首诗总共128行，用8年时间写成，体现诗人对默默无闻的农民的同情，惋惜他们没有机会施展天赋，同时也批评大人物的傲慢和奢侈。其对暮色中大自然的描写，对下层人民的同情感伤的情调，使该诗成为浪漫主义诗歌的先声，在艺术技巧上也达到古典主义诗艺的完美境界。从这首诗中，我们可以看到英国诗人从新古典主义向浪漫主义的过渡：一方面，格雷的诗歌语言精雕细琢，符合新古典主义推崇的诗歌词藻要求；另一方面，他的诗歌表现对自然以及对人与人之间和谐关系的渴望。

老虎

威廉·布莱克 著

导读：

《老虎》（*The Tiger*）是英国诗人威廉·布莱克（William Blake, 1757—1827）最著名的一首诗，收录在他的诗集《经验之歌》（*Songs of Experience*）中。这首诗由四行体扬抑格四音步构成，其音调铿锵有力，刻意在模仿打铁的声音。全诗由一系列的疑问句排列而成，表达诗人对神秘的造物主那巨大能量的惊讶和恐惧。

The Tiger

Tiger tiger burning bright,
In the forests of the night;
What immortal hand or eye,
Could frame thy fearful symmetry?

In what distant deeps or skies,
Burnt the fire of thine eyes?
On what wings dare he aspire?
What the hand dare seize the fire?

And what shoulder and what art,
Could twist the sinews of thy heart?
And when thy heart began to beat,
What dread hand and what dread feet?

What the hammer? What the chain?
In what furnace was thy brain?
What the anvil? What dread grasp,
Dare its deadly terrors clasp?

老虎老虎夜林里，
熊熊火光你燃起，
何种神手或天眼，
造你双目凶光显？

火光冒出你眼孔，
遥燃深渊或天空。
他乘何翼敢追击？
用何双手造虎眸？

以何技巧用何肩，
竟能把你心筋捻？
使你心脏可起伏，
何其强大手与足？

是何槌子是何链？
在何炉中你脑炼？
是何钢铁是何砧？
致命大钩胆敢抡？

When the stars threw down their spears,
And water'd heaven with their tears,
Did He smile His work to see?
Did He who made the lamb make thee?

Tiger tiger burning bright,
In the forests of the night.
What immortal hand or eye,
Dare frame thy fearful symmetry?

群星抛下其投枪。
用其眼泪润天堂,
他可笑看己作品?
他造羔羊亦造你?

老虎老虎夜林里,
熊熊火光你燃起,
何种神手或天眼,
造你双目凶光显?

爱德华·蒙克

《Head of an Old Man with Beard》

伦敦

威廉·布莱克 著

导读：

《伦敦》（*London*）是布莱克的著名短诗之一，诗人用这首诗揭露英国社会的种种腐败和罪恶，表达其对专制暴政的深恶痛绝。该诗从传统意义上说是在叙事，可从其时间线性上看，读者能找到其整体布置、发展。但作为既是诗人又是画家的布莱克，对其诗歌的欣赏，还可从绘画"空间"上进行探讨。本诗构建出"主题"和"静态"两个空间，空间不仅象征着诗歌叙事地点的切换，而且还能从中完成对诗歌结构与诗歌情感的渲染。所以，该诗可看作是诗歌艺术和绘画艺术的结合。

London

I wandered through each chartered street,
Near where the chartered Thames does flow,
And mark in every face I meet,
Marks of weakness, marks of woe.

In every cry of every man,
In every infant's cry of fear,
In every voice, in every ban,
The mind-forged manacles I hear:

How the chimney-sweeper's cry
Every blackening church appalls,
And the hapless soldier's sigh
Runs in blood down palace-walls.

But most, through midnight streets I hear
How the youthful harlot's curse
Blasts the new-born infant's tear,
And blights with plagues the marriage-hearse.

我走过每一条规划街道，
规划好的泰晤士河流过，
我看见每人脸上的表情，
人们显得既悲伤又衰弱。

每一个人的每一次呻吟，
每一回婴儿害怕的哭叫，
每一条禁令每一响声音，
都让我听到心铸的镣铐。

多少扫烟囱孩子的叫喊
震惊每一座阴暗的教堂，
而那些不幸兵士的长叹
化作鲜血流下宫殿围墙。

可最怕是深夜街头巷尾，
听多少年轻妓女在诅咒，
这诅咒盖住新生儿哭声，
如瘟疫般使婚车变灵柩。

鉴赏：

布莱克是英国重要的浪漫主义诗人、版画家，也是英国文学史上最重要的伟大诗人之一，同时他还是一位虔诚的基督教徒，一生都保持着宗教、政治和艺术上的激进倾向。他浓厚的宗教意识、艺术天分和丰富的人生阅历，给其诗歌提供取之不尽的创作源泉。其前期诗作主要包括《诗歌素描》《纯真之歌》《经验之歌》等。

布莱克前期的诗作，语言上简单易懂，且以短诗为主，音节也能短则短，题材内容则以生活中的所见所闻为主。诗集《纯真之歌》反对教会的禁欲观点，肯定生活和人生的美好，这与他反对专制、同情民主革命的思想息息相关。他对耶稣和天使的歌颂，则是出于其虔诚的基督教信仰。诗集《经验之歌》揭露英国政府和教会对童工和青少年的摧残，其中还有对被驱作战的士兵的叹息和贩卖女子为娼者的诅咒。布莱克后期的诗作明显增长，有时长达数百乃至上千行，内容也明显晦涩起来，富有神秘感和宗教气息，并充满了象征元素。

我像一朵云孤独地漫游

威廉·华兹华斯 著

导读：

《我像一朵云孤独地漫游》（*I Wandered Lonely as a Cloud*）是英国诗人威廉·华兹华斯（William Wordsworth, 1770—1850）的一首诗歌。本诗是其代表作之一。据说此诗是根据诗人和妹妹一起外出游玩时深深被大自然的美丽所吸引这一经历写成，体现诗人关于诗歌应描写"平静中回忆起来的情感"（emotion recollected in tranquility）这一诗学主张。全诗可分成两部分：写景与抒情。诗的开篇以第一人称叙述，格调显得低沉忧郁。诗人一方面竭力捕捉回忆的渺茫信息，另一方面享受独自漂游，因可以自由自在地欣赏大自然所赋予的美景。他把自己比作一朵流云，随意飘荡，富有想象的诗句暗示诗人有一种排遣孤独、向往自由的心情。在他的回忆中，水仙花缤纷茂密，如繁星点点在微风中轻盈飘舞。

I Wandered Lonely as a Cloud

I wandered lonely as a cloud
That floats on high o'er vales and hills,
When all at once I saw a crowd,
A host of golden daffodils;
Beside the lake, beneath the trees,
Fluttering and dancing in the breeze.

Continuous as the stars that shine
And twinkle on the Milky Way,
They stretched in never-ending line
Along the margin of a bay:
Ten thousand saw I at a glance,
Tossing their heads in sprightly dance.

The waves beside them danced, but they
Out-did the sparkling waves in glee;
A poet could not but be gay,
In such a jocund company;
I gazed—and gazed—but little thought
What wealth the show to me had brought:

我像一朵云孤独地漫游，
高高地飘浮在山谷之上，
忽然大片鲜花映入眼球，
原是金色水仙遍地开放，
开在湖畔也开在树根部，
随着微风飘荡翩翩起舞。

朵朵水仙恰似颗颗星星，
在那银河系中闪闪发光；
花朵沿着海湾边缘前行，
无休无止地延伸向前方；
放眼望去便有千朵万朵：
花儿搔首弄姿活泼起舞。

粼粼水波也在近旁狂欢，
可不如这水仙跳得欢快；
诗人有如此快乐的伙伴，
心情岂不为此变得开怀；
我久久凝视却几未感悟
此景带给我的竟是财富：

For oft, when on my couch I lie

In vacant or in pensive mood,

They flash upon that inward eye

Which is the bliss of solitude;

And then my heart with pleasure fills,

And dances with the daffodils.

因为每每我躺在长椅上，
感觉心灵空虚百无聊赖，
花儿即在眼前闪现光芒，
使我孤独的心无比欢快；
那刻我的心又充满乐趣，
便随着水仙跳欢乐舞曲。

鉴赏：

　　华兹华斯是英国浪漫主义诗人，曾当上桂冠诗人。其诗歌理论动摇英国古典主义诗学的统治，有力推动英国诗歌的革新和浪漫主义运动的发展。他是文艺复兴运动以来最重要的英语诗人之一，其诗句"朴素生活，高尚思考（plain living and high thinking）"被作为牛津大学基布尔学院的格言。

　　华兹华斯的小诗清丽，长诗清新而深刻，一反新古典主义平板、典雅的风格，开创新鲜活泼的浪漫主义诗风。《我像一朵云孤独地漫游》是其代表作之一。

忽必烈汗或梦中幻影

塞缪尔·泰勒·柯勒律治 著

导读：

《忽必烈汗或梦中幻影》(*Kubla Khan or a Vision in a Dream*)，是英国诗人塞缪尔·泰勒·柯勒律治（Samuel Taylor Coleridge, 1772—1834）的抒情诗。这首诗是他在1797年一个夏天梦中偶得之作。在这54行合辙押韵、长短不等、韵律铿锵的诗句中，诗人写道，他在埃克斯穆一个农庄小住时，由于身体不适，吃了鸦片不久便睡着。入睡前他正好在看珀切斯的一篇游记，其中谈到因马可波罗的介绍而在西方出名的元世祖忽必烈汗修建宫殿的事。诗人梦中将诗句脱口而出，纷至沓来，看到一系列形象，听到一连串写景状事的词句。几小时后他醒来，蛮有把握地认为自己已作好一首三百行左右的长诗。他想趁自己记得十分清晰，将长诗写下来。但一位不速之客打断他的工作，他忘记了许多，于是便只有现存的54行诗了。

Kubla Khan: or a Vision in a Dream

In Xanadu did Kubla Khan
A stately pleasure-dome decree:
Where Alph, the sacred river, ran
Through caverns measureless to man
   Down to a sunless sea.
So twice five miles of fertile ground
With walls and towers were girdled round;
And there were gardens bright with sinuous rills,
Where blossomed many an incense-bearing tree;
And here were forests ancient as the hills,
Enfolding sunny spots of greenery.

But oh! that deep romantic chasm which slanted
Down the green hill athwart a cedarn cover!
A savage place! as holy and enchanted
As e'er beneath a waning moon was haunted
By woman wailing for her demon-lover!
And from this chasm, with ceaseless turmoil seething,
As if this earth in fast thick pants were breathing,
A mighty fountain momently was forced:

忽必烈汗在上都曾下令，①
造座富丽堂皇的安乐宫：
此处阿方斯圣河在奔腾，
圣河穿过深不可测洞穴，
　流入阴暗的海底中。
于是方圆十英里的沃土，②
都围城墙盖起亭台楼屋：
在溪曲水清的园内建造，
园树鲜花吐露一片芬芳；
周边林地山冈同样古老，
围住日照的一块块草场。

啊！可那奇异的斜深壑，
沿青山横过伞形的柏树！
莽荒地神奇得令人着魔，
如同寡女淡月光下出没，
为她的恶魔恋人而哀哭！
壑下翻滚的水沸腾而起，
似地球在厚裤中急呼吸，
挤压出一股强大的喷泉：

121

Amid whose swift half-intermitted burst
Huge fragments vaulted like rebounding hail,
Or chaffy grain beneath the thresher's flail:
And 'mid these dancing rocks at once and ever
It flung up momently the sacred river.
Five miles meandering with a mazy motion
Through wood and dale the sacred river ran,
Then reached the caverns measureless to man,
And sank in tumult to a lifeless ocean;
And 'mid this tumult Kubla heard from far
Ancestral voices prophesying war!
  The shadow of the dome of pleasure
  Floated midway on the waves;
  Where was heard the mingled measure
  From the fountain and the caves.
It was a miracle of rare device,
A sunny pleasure-dome with caves of ice!

  A damsel with a dulcimer
  In a vision once I saw:
  It was an Abyssinian maid,
  And on her dulcimer she played,
  Singing of Mount Abora.
  Could I revive within me
  Her symphony and song,

泉水时断时续涌迸之间，
碎片跳跃像反弹的冰雹，
或像脱粒机下谷粒追跑：
那些岩石时不时舞动着，
突然从中涌出那条圣河。
河水幽幽十里蜿蜒流淌，
圣河在森林山谷里穿越，
然后流到深不可测洞穴，
喧嚣中注入寂静的海洋；
这时忽必烈远处闻此声：
祖先的呼喊预示着战争！

  安乐宫殿的那一片倒影
  在涟涟的水波中央浮动；
  那和谐的音韵诱人倾听，
  音韵传自那喷泉和岩洞。
日照的乐宫居然有冰窖，
创此奇迹可要罕见技巧！

  我于幻象曾见一个
  拿德西马琴的少女：
  阿比西尼亚的女仆，
  她在抚琴弹奏乐曲，
  她在歌唱阿博拉山。
  如果我心中能再唱

123

> To such a deep delight 't would win me,
> That with music loud and long,
> I would build that dome in air,
> That sunny dome! Those caves of ice!
> And all who heard should see them there,
> And all should cry, "Beware! Beware!
> His flashing eyes, his floating hair!
> Weave a circle round him thrice,
> And close your eyes with holy dread,
> For he on honey-dew hath fed,
> And drunk the milk of Paradise."

她的和谐曲和歌儿,
我将深感快乐无比,
用如此高亢悠长的乐曲,
在空中建造那座安乐殿,
即阳光照耀的宫殿冰窟!
闻乐者都该看到那些呀!
都该高喊当心呀当心呀!
都该看到他的乌发亮眼!
请坐一圈将他团团围住,
闭上你的双眼心怀敬畏,
因为他已把甘露来享用,
也已喝下那天堂的仙乳。

注释:

①上都:即元上都,位于广袤的内蒙古自治区锡林郭勒盟正蓝旗草原,是元王朝的首都,始建于公元1256年。它是中国大元王朝的发祥地,也是蒙元文化的发祥地,忽必烈在此登基建立元朝。"一座元上都,半部元朝史。"元朝的11位皇帝中,有6位皇帝是在上都登基。

②方圆十英里:元上都分外城、皇城和宫城三部分。外城整体呈曲尺形,围绕皇城之西、北两面扩建而成,西、北两面墙长2220米,东墙长815米,南墙长820米,占地面积约288公顷;皇城平面近方形,东墙长1410米,西墙长1415米,北墙长1395米,南墙长1400米,占地面积约164公顷;宫城平面近方形,东墙长605米,西墙长605.5米,北墙长542.5米,南墙长542米,占地面积约32公顷。

鉴赏：

　　柯勒律治是英国浪漫主义诗人、文艺批评家，湖畔派诗人代表。1795年与威廉·华兹华斯相遇并结成好友。3年后两人联合出版《抒情歌谣集》，开英国浪漫主义文学之先河。诗集收有《古舟子吟》等当时最美的诗歌。他还写有哲学、文艺批评的论著《文学传记》等。

　　柯勒律治的诗数量不多，但《古舟子咏》《克里斯特贝尔》和《忽必烈汗或梦中幻影》都脍炙人口，是英国诗歌中的瑰宝。这些诗显示柯勒律治创作的原则和特色，即以自然、逼真的形象和环境的描写表现超自然的、神圣的、浪漫的内容，使读者在阅读时产生信任感。

西风颂

珀西·比希·雪莱 著

导读：

《西风颂》（*Ode to the West Wind*）是珀西·比希·雪莱（Percy Bysshe Shelley，1792—1822）的"三大颂诗"之一，写于1819年。诗人用优美丰富的想象写出西风的形象。其气势恢宏的诗句，震撼人心的激情把西风的狂烈、横扫旧世界创造新世界的形象展现无遗；其奇特比喻与鲜明形象无不摄人心魄。最后两段，诗人与西风的应和令人心碎，道出诗人心灵的创伤。尽管如此，诗人愿意被西风吹拂，让自己即逝的生命在被撕碎的瞬间感受西风的气息，愿将自己的一切奉献给即将到来的春天。在诗结尾，诗人以预言家的口吻高喊：如果冬天来了，春天还远吗？诗人以西风自喻，表达自己对生活的信念和向旧世界宣战的决心。

Ode to the West Wind

1

O wild West Wind, thou breath of Autumn's being
Thou, from whose unseen presence the leaves dead
Are driven, like ghosts from an enchanter fleeing,

Yellow, and black, and pale, and hectic red,
Pestilence-stricken multitudes: O thou,
Who chariotest to their dark wintry bed

The winged seeds, where they lie cold and low,
Each like a corpse within its grave, until
Thine azure sister of the Spring shall blow

Her clarion o'er the dreaming earth, and fill
(Driving sweet buds like flocks to feed in air)
With living hues and odors plain and hill:

Wild Spirit, which art moving everywhere;
Destroyer and preserver; hear, oh, hear!

一

啊！西来狂风你是秋的气息，
来不见踪影的你让树叶凋零，
败叶像游魂从巫士手中逃离，

叶色或蜡黄黝黑或粉赤潮红，
也像得场瘟疫般往地上坠落。
啊，你给黑暗冬床慎播翼种，

却让其与冰冷的低洼地依偎，
粒粒种似具具尸在墓中埋掉，
直等到你那春天妹妹的蔚蓝

在梦幻般大地吹起春风号角，
让羊群在甜蜜花蕾空中觅食，
使得山川姹紫嫣红遍地香飘：

听吧，狂野精灵正四处飞奔；
既是保护使者又是破坏狂人！

2

Thou on whose stream, mid the steep sky's commotion,
Loose clouds like earth's decaying leaves are shed,
Shook from the tangled boughs of Heaven and Ocean,

Angels of rain and lightning: there are spread
On the blue surface of thine airy surge,
Like the bright hair uplifted from the head

Of some fierce Maenad, even from the dim verge
Of the horizon to the Zenith's height,
The locks of the approaching storm. Thou dirge

Of the dying year, to which this closing night
Will be the dome of a vast sepulchre,
Vaulted with all thy congregated might

Of vapours, from whose solid atmosphere
Black rain, and fire, and hail will burst: oh, hear!

3

Thou who didst waken from his summer dreams
The blue Mediterranean, where he lay,
Lulled by the coil of his crystalline streams,

二

在你那高空的滚滚气流上方，
乱云像地上枯叶一般被吹散，
抖落下海天相接的树枝头上，

乱云像天使把雨水闪电携带，
在气流翻腾的碧蓝海面散花；
就像从一些凶猛的狂女脑袋

被吹起的那一缕缕金色头发，
甚至从朦胧地平线到天顶盖，
你把即将来临的暴风雨钳夹，

你是残年挽歌而在夜幕降时，
夜空形成那一座大墓的圆顶，
被蒸汽凝聚的一切力量拱起，

听吧！从这团凝聚的气层中，
黑雨、电火和冰雹即将喷涌。

三

你确实曾唤醒过蓝色地中海，
他躺在拜伊海湾里的浮岛边，
在夏日幻梦般的海景上感慨，

Beside a pumice isle in Baiae's bay,
And saw in sleep old palaces and towers
Quivering within the eave's intenser day,

All overgrown with azure moss and flowers
So sweet, the sense faints picturing them! Thou
For whose path the Atlantic's level powers

Cleave themselves into chasms, while far below
The sea-blooms and the oozy woods which wear
The sapless foliage of the ocean, know

Thy voice, and suddenly grow gray with fear,
And tremble and despoil themselves: oh, hear!

4

If I were a dead leaf thou mightest bear;
If I were a swift cloud to fly with thee;
A wave to pant beneath thy power, and share

The impulse of thy strength, only less free
Than thou, O uncontrollable! If even
I were as in my boyhood, and could be

The comrade of thy wanderings over Heaven,

受到那一圈晶莹水流的催眠，
睡梦中见到古老的宫殿楼阁，
晃动在屋檐下更强的日光间，

都长满蓝色苔藓并充满花香，
甜甜的花香味令人难以描述！
大西洋风平浪静的海水力量，

因你的开路从海面直劈海底，
海花和海底深处的淤泥丛林，
全都披上大海中枯萎的叶子，

它们听到你的声音大惊失色，
啊！且听海花凋谢丛林抖瑟。

四

如果我是你能忍的一片败叶；
如果我是随你飞的一朵流云；
既是在你威风下的急急喘歇，

又是享受你脉动的一朵浪花，
只是不比你自由且难以驾驭！
纵然我好像处在孩提的年华，

能够陪伴你肆意漫游在天空，

133

As then, when to outstrip thy skyey speed
Scarce seemed a vision; I would ne'er have striven

As thus with thee in prayer in my sore need.
Oh, lift me as a wave, a leaf, a cloud!
I fall upon the thorns of life! I bleed!

A heavy weight of hours has chained and bowed
One too like thee: tameless, and swift, and proud.

5

Make me thy lyre, even as the forest is:
What if my leaves are falling like its own!
The tumult of thy mighty harmonies

Will take from both a deep, autumnal tone,
Sweet though in sadness. Be thou, Spirit fierce,
My spirit! Be thou me, impetuous one!

Drive my dead thoughts over the universe
Like withered leaves to quicken a new birth!
And, by the incantation of this verse,

Scatter, as from an unextinguished hearth
Ashes and sparks, my words among mankind!

那时一样比你飞快似非幻想；
在我为强烈的需要而祈祷中，

我决不会因此与你进行抗争，
让我像一浪一叶一云朵高飞！
我遭遇人生棘刺而鲜血直淌！

时光重负束缚像你一样的人：
难以驯服且疾速高傲地飞奔。

五

把我当你的竖琴甚至当树丛，
即便叶子正在凋零那又何妨？
我们在你强烈和谐的骚动中，

虽然悲伤却以秋的深沉音调，
甜美地歌唱你是凶猛的精灵，
精灵呀！让我像你那样狂飙。

把我僵死的思想驱散在宇宙，
就像驱散加快催生片片枯叶！
那么请你按照诗篇中的符咒，

把我所说的话为全人类传递，
犹如熄灭炉膛吹出烟灰火花！

Be through my lips to unawakened earth

The trumpet of a prophecy! O Wind,
If Winter comes, can Spring be far behind?

用我的嘴唇对着沉睡的大地，

吹出一段预言的号角：风啊！
如果冬天来了，春天还远吗？

鉴赏：

　　雪莱，英国浪漫主义民主诗人、第一位社会主义诗人、小说家、哲学家、散文家、政论作家、改革家、柏拉图主义者和理想主义者，其受空想社会主义思想影响颇深。他是英国文学史上有才华的抒情诗人之一，被誉为"诗人中的诗人"，与乔治·戈登·拜伦并称为英国浪漫主义诗歌的"双子星"。

　　雪莱爱幻想、富有浪漫主义气质。因此，他的诗作总是洋溢着瑰丽广博的想象。正是这种高超的想象力，丰富他的诗歌内容，使其风格迥异，意境开阔。在他富有想象的抒情诗作中，《西风颂》节奏明快，音律和谐，气势豪放，想象瑰丽，令读者心旷神怡，浮想联翩。这首诗充分体现雪莱富于想象的创作手法。《西风颂》共五节。在第一、二节中，雪莱运用丰富的想象，生动地书写狂暴的西风雄浑磅礴的气势，表现西风摧枯拉朽，所向披靡，摧毁旧世界，开拓新世界的强大威力。第三节中，雪莱承前呼应，以高超的想象，淋漓尽致地描绘西风驱卷天空的浮云，威震地中海，斩劈大西洋的壮阔画面与威猛气势。第四、五节，诗人更是浮想翩翩，将自己引入诗的意境，与西风融为一体，让西风把他的思绪拨散人间。雪莱借用想象，把自己的情感寄托在客观事物中，清晰明了地表达自己的革命理想。这种奇思异想、托物写意的文学表现手法，为诗作增添不少光彩。

夜莺颂

约翰·济慈 著

导读：

《夜莺颂》（*Ode to a Nightingale*）是约翰·济慈（John Keats，1759—1821）的诗作。全诗共八节。开篇写诗人听闻莺歌后，置身瑰丽的幻想境界。继而写自己纵饮美酒，诗兴大发，凭诗遐想，随夜莺飘然而去，深夜醉卧花丛，缕缕芳香袭面而来。这时，诗人陶然自乐，心旷神怡，愿就此离别人世。人都有一死，而夜莺的歌却永世不灭。想到此，诗人梦幻结束，重返现实。在济慈看来，他生活于其中的社会是庸俗、虚伪、污浊、肮脏的，而永恒的大自然则绮丽秀美、清新可爱。对丑的鞭挞和对美的追求构成他抒情诗的基调。

Ode to a Nightingale

1

My heart aches, and a drowsy numbness pains
   My sense, as though of hemlock I had drunk,
Or emptied some dull opiate to the drains
   One minute past, and Lethe-wards had sunk:
'Tis not through envy of thy happy lot,
   But being too happy in thine happiness, —
      That thou, light winged Dryad of the trees,
         In some melodious plot
Of beechen green, and shadows numberless,
      Singest of summer in full-throated ease.

2

O, for a draught of vintage! that hath been
   Cool'd a long age in the deep-delved earth,
Tasting of Flora and the country green,
   Dance, and Provencal song, and sunburnt mirth!
O for a beaker full of the warm South
   Full of the true, the blushful Hippocrene,
      With beaded bubbles winking at the brim,

一

心疼得四肢麻木昏欲睡，
　我感觉像是喝下了毒芹，
或像服了些干燥鸦片碎，
　一分钟后忘川病房已沉：
这不是我妒忌你的福气，
　而是你快乐使我太快乐——
　　你是那羽翼翩翩的树精，
　　　在歌声悠扬之地，
绿榉树中无数阴影掩遮，
为唱响夏天你放声高歌。

二

啊，多希望有美酒佳酿，
　痛饮深窖冷藏多年美酒，
品花神酒后念绿色酒乡，
　想舞恋歌且狂欢思未休！
啊，要是酒飘南国热气，
　充满真正令人羞愧灵泉，
　　珍珠般泡沫在杯沿闪动，

141

        And purple-stained mouth,
That I might drink, and leave the world unseen,
    And with thee fade away into the forest dim.

3

Fade far away, dissolve, and quite forget
    What thou amongst the leaves hast never known,
The weariness, the fever, and the fret
    Here, where men sit and hear each other groan;
Where palsy shakes a few, sad, last grey hairs,
    Where youth grows pale, and spectre-thin, and dies;
        Where but to think is to be full of sorrow
            And leaden-eyed despairs;
Where Beauty cannot keep her lustrous eyes,
        Or new Love pine at them beyond to-morrow.

4

Away! Away! For I will fly to thee,
    Not charioted by Bacchus and his pards,
But on the viewless wings of Poesy,
    Though the dull brain perplexes and retards.
Already with thee! Tender is the night,
    And haply the Queen-Moon is on her throne,
        Clustered around by all her starry Fays;
            But here there is no light,

把嘴唇染得粉赤，
我喝后能悄然离开世间，
随你消失在幽暗的林中。

三

远远隐没消失且全忘掉
　　你树叶间从不知的东西，
忘掉在此的倦烦与烦忧，
　　这里人们坐听彼此叹息；
瘫者最后几根白发摇晃，
　　青春变苍老瘦削至逝世；
　　　人们想到此便满怀伤悲，
　　　　沉重双眼陷绝望；
这儿美人双眸难保明丽，
或者新欢明日即将告吹。

四

飞吧！因为我要飞向你，
　　不与酒神驾驶豹车同行，
而要乘上诗神无形双翼。
　　尽管迷惑呆滞大脑僵硬，
柔和夜色下我和你同在！
月亮皇后快乐登上宝座，
　　被她所有星星仙子簇拥；
　　　可这儿没有光亮，

Save what from heaven is with the breezes blown
>> Through verdurous glooms and winding mossy ways.

5

I cannot see what flowers are at my feet,
> Nor what soft incense hangs upon the boughs,

But, in embalmed darkness, guess each sweet
> Wherewith the seasonable month endows

The grass, the thicket, and the fruit-tree wild—
>> White hawthorn, and the pastoral eglantine;
>> Fast fading violets covered up in leaves;
>> And mid-May's eldest child,
>>> The coming musk-rose, full of dewy wine,
>> The murmurous haunt of flies on summer eves.

6

Darkling I listen; and for many a time
> I have been half in love with easeful Death,

Called him soft names in many a mused rhyme,
> To take into the air my quiet breath;

Now more than ever seems it rich to die,
To cease upon the midnight with no pain,
>> While thou art pouring forth thy soul abroad
>>> In such an ecstasy!

Still wouldst thou sing, and I have ears in vain—

除天光外只有微风吹过,
吹过绿幽处吹过苔曲径。

五

无法看到脚下是什么花,
　无法看到什么软香挂枝,
可馨夜中猜想每种芬华
　在其每一个时令月赋予
小草灌木,赋予野生树果,
　亦赋予山楂和野生玫瑰;
　　早凋紫罗兰被绿叶遮蔽;
　　　五月中旬的骄儿,
含苞麝香玫瑰飘酒香味,
它是夏夜蚊蝇飞嗡之地。

六

在黑暗中倾听你的歌声,
　多次几将静谧死神爱恋。
多以诗韵呼唤他的美称,
　求他把我生命化作青烟。
现在似乎更感死的风采,
　以求午夜离尘世痛可免,
　　在此刻你是如此狂喜地
　　　直接抒出你情怀,
你愿高唱可我不再听见——

145

To thy high requiem become a sod.

7

Thou wast not born for death, immortal Bird!
  No hungry generations tread thee down;
The voice I hear this passing night was heard
  In ancient days by emperor and clown:
Perhaps the self-same song that found a path
  Through the sad heart of Ruth, when, sick for home,
    She stood in tears amid the alien corn;
      The same that oft-times hath
Charm'd magic casement, opening on the foam
  Of perilous seas, in faery lands forlorn.

8

Forlorn! the very word is like a bell
  To toll me back from thee to my sole self!
Adieu! the fancy cannot cheat so well
  As she is famed to do, deceiving elf.
Adieu! adieu! thy plaintive anthem fades
  Past the near meadows, over the still stream,
    Up the hill-side; and now 'tis buried deep
      In the next valley-glades:
Was is a vision, or a waking dream?
    Fled is that music—Do I wake or sleep?

高亢的安魂曲献给草皮。

七

永生的灵鸟你生而不死!
　代代饥饿无法把你压倒;
这个夜晚我听到的歌词,
　也为古代帝王、庶民闻知晓:
或许同首歌寻觅一条路,
　通往那露丝哀思的家乡,
　　她站在陌生玉米地嚎啕,
　　　同样的事情常出,
孤寂仙境中她伫立魔窗,
推开危海上的骇浪惊涛。

八

孤寂!这歌词宛如洪钟,
　唤我从你那儿回归自我。
再见!幻想如骗人妖精,
　可不像盛传那样的高明。
再见!再见!哀歌渐逝,
　越过附近草地越过静流,
　　越过山坡之下的山谷内,
　　　那歌声完全消失:
这是个幻影还是白日梦?
歌声远去——我是醒是睡?

爱德华·蒙克

《女孩点燃火炉》

希腊古瓮颂

约翰·济慈 著

导读:

《希腊古瓮颂》(*Ode on a Grecian Urn*)是济慈对美的颂歌。该诗通过诗人对古瓮的观感以及与古瓮的对话,得出"美即是真,真即是美"的结论。诗中古瓮之美在于"优雅"和"美妙",此美是艺术之美。这首诗和古瓮是美的,美源自有悲也有乐的生活,这便是真。生活的本真是艺术美的源泉,艺术美使生活本真得以永存。济慈的艺术成就是他在生活本真中追求美的结果,他所创造出来的艺术美使他的一生不朽于世。

Ode on a Grecian Urn

1

Thou still unravish'd bride of quietness,
   Thou foster-child of silence and slow time,
Sylvan historian, who canst thus express
   A flowery tale more sweetly than our rhyme:
What leaf-fring'd legend haunts about thy shape
    Of deities or mortals, or of both,
      In Tempe or the dales of Arcady?
    What men or gods are these? What maidens loath?
What mad pursuit? What struggle to escape?
      What pipes and timbrels? What wild ecstasy?

2

Heard melodies are sweet, but those unheard
   Are sweeter; therefore, ye soft pipes, play on;
Not to the sensual ear, but, more endear'd,
   Pipe to the spirit ditties of no tone:
Fair youth, beneath the trees, thou canst not leave
    Thy song, nor ever can those trees be bare;
      Bold Lover, never, never canst thou kiss,

一

你依然是个安静的童贞姑娘,
　　也是"沉默"与"悠久"抚育的养女,
像乡村史家那样能如此来讲
　　比我们的诗句还甜美的童话:
你的身材是缠叶的古老传说,
　　在谈述神明或是在叙说凡人,
　　　　人神在坦佩或在世外山谷里?
何为这人这神?何为少女恨?
何为疯狂追求?为何拼命躲?
　　　　何为风笛与鼓?为何疯狂喜?

二

听到的旋律甜美,可未听到
　　的更美;所以,吹起柔笛吧;
不是吹给耳听,而是更钟爱,
　　对着灵魂吹奏出无调的小曲:
树下的美少年呀你不能停唱
　　你的歌,而树绝不能光秃秃;
　　　　大胆的恋人永无法将你吻到,

Though winning near the goal—yet, do not grieve;
　She cannot fade, though thou hast not thy bliss,
　　For ever wilt thou love, and she be fair!

3

Ah, happy, happy boughs! that cannot shed
　Your leaves, nor ever bid the Spring adieu;
And, happy melodist, unwearied,
　For ever piping songs for ever new;
More happy love! more happy, happy love!
　For ever warm and still to be enjoy'd,
　　For ever panting, and for ever young;
　All breathing human passion far above,
That leaves a heart high—sorrowful and cloyed,
　　A burning forehead, and a parching tongue.

4

Who are these coming to the sacrifice?
　To what green altar, O mysterious priest,
Lead'st thou that heifer lowing at the skies,
　And all her silken flanks with garlands drest?
What little town by river or sea shore,
　Or mountain—built with peaceful citadel,
　　Is emptied of this folk, this pious morn?
　And, little town, thy streets for evermore

虽够近目标——可不必悲伤；
你虽不能如愿，但她不衰老，
　　你将永爱下去，她貌美如初！

三

啊，幸福的树枝！它既不掉
　　它枝叶，也从不曾离开春天；
幸福的吹笛人并不感到疲劳，
　　他吹奏的歌曲永远那么新鲜；
更幸福的爱！无比幸福的爱！
　　仍让情人享受，永远地热情，
　　　　永远地在渴望，葆青春本色；
所有生活者的激情无比澎湃，
那却给心里留下悲伤和阴影，
　　也留下灼热的额和炽热的舌。

四

这些赶着去祭祀的人都是谁？
　　那只小母牛正对着天空叫哭，
她丝般光滑的侧腹花环满缀，
　　神秘的祭司你牵母牛到哪处？
是从哪个河边或海边的小镇，
　　还是从哪个山上幽静的城堡，
　　　　在这敬神场合，这些人聚此处？
然而小镇，你的街永将寂闷，

Will silent be; and not a soul to tell
    Why thou art desolate, can e'er return.

5

O Attic shape! Fair attitude! with brede
    Of marble men and maidens overwrought,
With forest branches and the trodden weed;
    Thou, silent form, dost tease us out of thought
As doth eternity: Cold Pastoral!
    When old age shall this generation waste,
        Thou shalt remain, in midst of other woe
        Than ours, a friend to man, to whom thou say'st,
"Beauty is truth, truth beauty,"—that is all
    Ye know on earth, and all ye need to know.

再也不可能有一个人把头调,
　　回来告诉人们你为什么孤独。

五

阁楼的造型呀！优美的姿势！
　楼面上镶嵌石雕的忧郁男女,
周边有林木和践踏过的青草;
　你无声的形体犹如永恒之作,
你想取笑我们：寒冷的牧歌!
　当暮年即将使这一代人没落,
　　你仍比我们其他人忧伤多些,
　并且以朋友的口吻对人们说：
美即是真,真即是美——这
　　包含世上你所知、该知的一切。

爱德华·蒙克

《Harpy》

致秋天

约翰·济慈 著

导读：

《致秋天》(*To Autumn*) 是济慈晚期的诗歌，诗人具有丰富的想象力，而且善于将人类的感官转化为绝美的文字，能够写透人乃至动物的心灵。这首诗在主客体关系、诗歌的写作风格和诗人的思想意识等方面，突出表现自我与客观世界、想象与纯真自然、写实与诗意相融合的审美观。诗歌同时表现了诗人在朴素、自然的生命形式中，对人文精神的追求。这使得本诗具备超越唯美主义的内在品格，与现代主义的美学思想交相辉映。

Spares the next swath and all its twined flowers;
And sometimes like a gleaner thou dost keep;
Steady thy laden head across a brook;
Or by a cider-press, with patient look,
    Thou watchest the last oozings hours by hours.

3

Where are the songs of Spring? Ay, where are they?
    Think not of them, thou hast thy music too, —
While barred clouds bloom the soft-dying day,
    And touch the stubble-plains with rosy hue;
Then in a wailful choir the small gnats mourn
    Among the river—sallows, borne aloft
Or sinking as the light wind lives or dies;
    And full-grown lambs loud bleat from hilly bourn;
Hedge-crickets sing; and now with treble soft
    The red-breast whistles from a garden-croft;
And gathering swallows twitter in the skies.

留出一畦庄稼和成对的花草；
有时你好像一个人在拾谷穗，
头顶一筐谷穗蹚过一条小溪，
或站在榨汁机旁连续数小时
耐心看完最后几滴浆汁流好。

三

春天之歌在哪里啊？在哪里？
别想它们，因为你有你的歌——
温暖的一天渐尽凝云舒展时，
长满残茎的田野变成玫瑰色；
各种小虫组成悲伤的合唱团，
在河畔的柳树林中高唱哀调，
歌声随着轻风起伏时高时低；
大羊羔在丘陵小溪咩声高远，
树篱的蟋蟀在歌唱而知更鸟
此时在园里轻声细语地鸣叫，
成群的燕子在空中叽叽喳喳。

鉴赏：

济慈是19世纪初期英国诗人、浪漫派的主要成员，1818年到1820年先后完成《夜莺颂》《希腊古瓮颂》《致秋天》等作品。他与雪莱、拜伦齐名，被推崇为欧洲浪漫主义运动的代表。

爱与美是济慈毕生的精神追求。虽然他短暂的一生中充满"疲劳、热病"，但他仍旧在长诗中构筑一个爱与美交织的世界。诗人在《夜莺颂》中，淋漓尽致地表现出现实中的冲突与悲痛。该诗一开始描写主人公身处的洋溢着欢歌笑语的精彩世界。夜莺在大自然中无牵无挂快乐鸣叫，将生活的美妙用婉转的歌声来表达。听到鸟儿的歌唱，主人公一开始喜出望外，紧接着悲从中来：他被病魔折磨得苦不堪言，听到了夜莺快乐的歌唱，对比自己的处境难免心生悲伤。尽管诗人创作的咏物诗十分少见，但该类诗歌在他的作品中占有很重要的地位，其中包括《希腊古瓮颂》。《希腊古瓮颂》不但描写古瓮的外形特征，还着力表现雕刻在上面的画作，济慈将咏物、写景、抒情都融于一体，使整部作品彰显出别具一格的艺术魅力。济慈在其中提出"美即是真，真即是美"这个命题，对后世抒情诗创作影响较大。

康科德之歌

拉尔夫·瓦尔多·爱默生 著

导读：

《康科德之歌》(*Concord Hymn*)是美国超验主义诗人拉尔夫·瓦尔多·爱默生（Ralph Waldo Emerson，1803—1882）的诗作，是美国文学中最负盛名的诗章之一。爱默生的超验主义思想与距波士顿西边仅32公里的一个新英格兰小村庄康科德（Concord）有着密切联系。康科德是原马萨诸塞湾殖民地的首个内陆定居点，四周森林环抱，从古至今幽静安详，距波士顿的书店和大学很近，因此其文化气息浓厚，但同时又远离尘嚣。康科德是美国独立战争首次战役的战场，爱默生曾赋诗纪念这场战斗。

Concord Hymn

By the rude bridge that arched the flood,
Their flag to April's breeze unfurled,
Here once the embattled farmers stood
And fired the shot heard round the world.

The foe long since in silence slept;
Alike the conqueror silent sleeps;
And Time the ruined bridge has swept
Down the dark stream which seaward creeps.

On this green bank, by this soft stream,
We set to-day a votive stone;
That memory may their deed redeem,
When, like our sires, our sons are gone.

Spirit, that made those heroes dare
To die, and leave their children free,
Bid Time and Nature gently spare
The shaft we raise to them and thee.

在那座简陋的拦水桥边,
旗帜迎着四月微风飘扬,
农夫曾严阵以待于前线,
打响全球听到的那一枪。

敌人们早已经在此长眠,
征服者也悄然进入梦乡;
那座桥却已被时光摧毁,
桥下暗河缓缓流向海洋。

水流旁边的翠绿河岸上,
我们现将一座石碑竖起;
子孙万代都像我们那样,
能铭记他们的丰功伟绩。

让英雄勇于赴死的精神,
将自由留给他们的后辈,
时光大地静静见证尘寰,
我们为你们和他们树碑。

文森特·梵高

《Railway Carriages》

梵天

拉尔夫·瓦尔多·爱默生 著

导读：

《梵天》(*Brahma*)发表在《大西洋月刊》创刊号上（1857年），使不熟悉梵天（印度教最高神）以及永恒无限的宇宙精神的读者感到困惑。爱默生给读者的建议是："让他们说耶和华，而不是梵天。"爱默生的精神视野和现实的、格言式的表达给读者以欢愉；康科德的一位超验主义者曾非常恰当地将聆听爱默生的作品比作"在秋千上荡入天堂"。他的许多灵性洞见来自对东方宗教的阅读，特别是印度教以及伊斯兰苏菲派经典学说。例如在这首诗中，他借助印度教宣扬超越肉体感官的宇宙秩序。

Brahma

If the red slayer think he slays,
Or if the slain think he is slain,
They know not well the subtle ways
I keep, and pass, and turn again.

Far or forgot to me is near;
Shadow and sunlight are the same;
The vanished gods to me appear;
And one to me are shame and fame.

They reckon ill who leave me out;
When me they fly, I am the wings;
I am the doubter and the doubt,
I am the hymn the Brahmin sings.

The strong gods pine for my abode,
And pine in vain the sacred Seven;
But thou, meek lover of the good!
Find me, and turn thy back on heaven.

若血腥杀者以为他杀人，
若被杀者以为他遭杀害，
他们尚不知我细微窍门，
我坚持超越并转身重来。

遥远或遗忘皆在我身边，
阴影以及阳光不无二致，
消失神明会在眼前出现，
耻辱与声誉于我融一体。

他们恶意以为会离开我，
飞翔时我是他们的羽翼；
我既是疑者也是那疑惑，
我是僧侣歌唱的赞美诗。

大神渴望得到我的住处，
七圣徒更有徒劳的愿望。
可你却是谦卑善良情夫！
找到我你转身背对天堂。

爱德华·霍普

《Office in a Small City》

日子

拉尔夫·瓦尔多·爱默生 著

导读：

《日子》(*Days*)是爱默生创作的一首诗歌。该诗在结构上明显分为两层，前面六行是对时间机制的人格化描述，后面五行则是"我"在这种机制中的个人化表现。对时间流逝的惋惜其实是由于惶恐失去自我，1851年的爱默生已经奠定他的超验主义领袖地位，可不管对谁来说，"消除那些使自我失去自己的隐蔽和阴暗的东西"都是一个远未结束的过程。时间是自我的基石，也是自我的深渊，在克服一次"沉沦"之后将面临新的"沉沦"。

Days

Daughters of Time, the hypocritic Days,
Muffled and dumb like barefoot dervishes,
And marching single in an endless file,
Bring diadems and faggots in their hands.
To each they offer gifts after his will,
Bread, kingdoms, stars, and sky that holds them all.
I, in my pleached garden, watched the pomp,
Forgot my morning wishes, hastily
Took a few herbs and apples, and the Day
Turned and departed silent. I, too late,
Under her solemn fillet saw the scorn.

光阴的女儿与伪善的日子,
喑哑无言得就像赤脚苦僧,
独行于没有尽头的队列中,
他们头戴皇冠且手拄权杖,
随心所愿向众生赠送礼品,
送食送国送星送万象天空。
我在枝缠的花园观看盛况,
竟然忘了自己清晨的愿望,
匆忙采摘一些香草和苹果,
在日转消逝的庄严头带下,
我迟迟才看出时光的轻蔑。

鉴赏：

　　爱默生，美国思想家、文学家、诗人，是确立美国文化精神的代表人物，也是新英格兰超验主义最杰出的代言人。美国总统林肯称他为"美国的孔子""美国文明之父"。其代表作品有《论自然》《美国学者》等，《论自然》被认为是新英格兰超验主义的圣经，而《美国学者》被誉为"美国思想文化领域的独立宣言"。

　　爱默生集散文作家、思想家、诗人于一身。他的诗歌独具特色，注重思想内容，没有过分华丽的辞藻，行文犹如格言，哲理深入浅出，说服力强，且有典型的"爱默生风格"。有人如此评价他"爱默生似乎只写警句"。其文字所透出的气质难以形容：既充满专制式的不容置疑，又具有开放式的民主精神；既有贵族式的傲慢，更具有平民式的直接；既清晰易懂，又常常夹杂着某种神秘主义……一个人能在一篇文章中塞入那么多的警句实在是了不起的，那些值得在清晨诵读的句子总能够振奋人心。岁月不是为他蒙上灰尘，而是映衬得他熠熠闪光。

生命的礼赞

亨利·沃兹沃斯·朗费罗 著

导读：

《生命的礼赞》(*A Psalm of Life*)这首诗是19世纪美国诗人亨利·沃兹沃斯·朗费罗（Henry Wadsworth Longfellow, 1807—1882）的代表作。该诗是在其前妻去世之后创作的。朗费罗的感情道路十分坎坷，前妻去世后，他伤心不已，向第二任妻子的求爱道路，又一波三折。于是，朗费罗创作这首诗。整首诗带给人们以正面的引导，告诉人们即使身处逆境，也不要灰心丧气，而要振作起精神，对生活抱乐观积极的态度。

A Psalm of Life

Tell me not in mournful numbers,
Life is but an empty dream!
For the soul is dead that slumbers,
And things are not what they seem.

Life is real! Life is earnest!
And the grave is not its goal;
Dust thou art, to dust returnest,
Was not spoken of the soul.

Not enjoyment, and not sorrow,
Is our destined end or way;
But to act, that each tomorrow
Finds us farther than today.

Art is long, and Time is fleeting,
And our hearts, though stout and brave,
Still, like muffled drums, are beating
Funeral marches to the grave.

别用悲伤的语调对我倾诉：
生命只是幻梦般的空魂！
因为沉睡的灵魂已经作古，
万物并非其显现的原本。

生命本真实！生命本严肃！
生命的终点绝不是墓坟；
你虽来自尘土也归于尘土，
可这是说肉体而非灵魂。

我们注定的结局抑或道路，
既不是享受也不是悔恨；
而是为每一个明天的付出，
见证我们比今日走更远。

艺术本长久而时光逝飞速，
我们虽有英勇顽强之心，
可心像一面面低沉的乐鼓，
正朝着坟墓将哀乐低吟。

In the world's broad field of battle,
In the bivouac of Life,
Be not like dumb, driven cattle!
Be a hero in the strife!

Trust no future, howe'er pleasant!
Let the dead Past bury its dead!
Act—act in the living Present!
Heart within, and God o'erhead!

Lives of great men all remind us
We can make our lives sublime,
And, departing, leave behind us
Footprints on the sands of time;

Footprints that perhaps another,
Sailing o'er life's solemn main,
A forlorn and shipwrecked brother,
Seeing, shall take heart again.

Let us, then, be up and doing,
With a heart for any fate;
Still achieving, still pursuing,
Learn to labour and to wait.

在世界的辽阔战场上露宿，
在这片生命的野营住屯，
别作任人驱使的沉默牲畜，
要在战斗中当一名战神！

未来再美好也莫于斯托付！
让过去的亡者将死侵吞！
行动——在此时此刻行动！
胸中有红心头顶有天神！

伟人的生命都让我们记住：
我们能使生命变得超伦，
然后离世时在我们身后处，
在时间沙滩上留下脚印。

也许是另一位弟兄的脚步，
在生命的庄严大海起航，
不幸遇难时足迹映入双目，
这将使人内心再扬风帆。

那让我们动起来心往一处，
以迎接任何命运的降临；
我们还在作为并不断追逐，
请学会劳动并学会等待。

To Helen

Helen, thy beauty is to me
Like those Nicean barks of yore,
That gently, o'er a perfumed sea,
The weary, wayworn wanderer bore
To his own native shore.

On desperate seas long wont to roam,
Thy hyacinth hair, thy classic face,
Thy Naiad airs have brought me home
To the glory that was Greece,
And the grandeur that was Rome.

Lo! in yon brilliant window-niche
How statue-like I see thee stand,
The agate lamp within thy hand!
Ah, Psyche, from the regions which
Are Holy Land!

海伦，你的美貌在我眼里，
犹如昔日尼西亚①的三桅帆，
船在飘香的大海悠然漂移，
将厌烦漂泊的那疲倦船员
送回故乡的岸边。

早已习惯在绝望大海荡划，
你有飘飘长发，古典面孔，
你以女神的风范带我回家，
进入属于希腊的光荣，
进入属于罗马的宏大。

看哪！明亮的窗式壁龛里，
我看你站着多像一尊雕像，
一盏玛瑙灯拿在你的手上！
啊，塞姬②，这神圣的土地
才是你的故乡！

注释：

①尼西亚（Nicaea）：历史上重要的古城，今为土耳伊兹尼克（Iznik）市。

②塞姬（Psyche）：希腊神话中人的灵魂化身，爱神厄洛斯为她的美貌所倾倒并最终娶她为妻。

安娜贝尔·李

埃德加·爱伦·坡 著

导读：

美国抒情诗中的上乘佳作《安娜贝尔·李》（*Annabel Lee*），是爱伦·坡1849年死后才发表的最后一篇诗作，代表其唯美主义风格的顶峰。许多评论家认为该诗是诗人为悼念亡妻而作，旨在把爱情融入理想化的永恒境界。全诗浓笔渲染大海边亦真亦幻的浪漫氛围，既有纯洁的爱情，也有哀婉的悲剧。大海的波涛传递悲切的旋律。全诗情景交融，音乐和画面和谐，鲜明的视觉形象和忧郁抒情节奏，生动形象地演绎了一个爱情传奇，委婉感人地抒发诗人缠绵悲伤的心情，呈现给读者的是美的意境，美的人物，美的故事，美的感情，美的韵律以及美的语言。

In this kindom by the sea.

The angels, not half so happy in the Heaven,
   Went evnying her and me
Yes! That was the reason (as all men know,
   in this kingdom by the sea)
That the wind came out of the cloud by night,
   Chilling and killing my Annabel Lee.

But our love it was stronger by far than the love
   Of those who were older than we—
   Of many far wiser than we—
And neither the angels in heaven above,
   Nor the demons down under the sea,
Can ever dissever my soul from the soul
   Of the beautiful Annabel Lee;

For the moon never beams without bringing me dreams
   Of the beautiful Annalbel Lee;
And the stars never rise, but I see the bright eyes
   Of the beautiful Annabel Lee;
And so, all the night-tide, I lie down by the side
Of my darling—my darling—my life and my bride,
   In the sepulchre there by the sea,
   In her tomb by the sounding sea.

关在这海洋的国度里。

天使们不及我们一半快乐,
　　在天堂把我和她妒忌,
对!是这个缘故(谁都懂,
　　在这个海洋的国度里)
夜晚从云端刮起那一阵风,
　　把安娜贝尔·李冻死。

可我们有过的爱情远胜过
　　那些年长于我们的人——
　　那些比我们智慧的人——
无论是天使在高高的天国,
　　还是恶魔在深深海底,
都不可能分离我们的灵魂,
　　我和安娜贝尔·李。

因为月光总会带给我一场场梦,
　　梦到美丽的安娜贝尔·李;
繁星升起无不让我看到她明眸,
　　那是美丽的安娜贝尔·李;
就这样伴着夜潮我躺在她身旁,
亲爱的,我的生命,我的新娘,
　　就在大海边的那座坟茔里,
　　就在大海旁边她的墓穴里。

鉴赏：

爱伦·坡，19世纪美国诗人、小说家和文学评论家，美国浪漫主义思潮的重要成员。他的文艺思想深受英国诗人和文艺理论家柯勒律治的影响，后自成一体，他的创作实践则完全反映他的文学理论。坡提出诗歌要写"美"的唯美主义美学原则。坡认为："美是诗的唯一正统的领域"，获得美感是艺术的最终目的。诗歌不是客观现实的反映，"其直接目的，与科学不同，不是真，而是快感"，一首诗歌不应充满道德说教的意味，应只是灵魂的"强烈而纯净的激动"，是属于"彼岸"的"神圣美"。因此，诗人的创作不应追求其社会功能，而应"为诗而诗"，诗歌应是一种"激情"，而不应是为某一"目的"。

坡作为美国浪漫主义早期诗人，其深远的影响在于他和现代象征派诗人在许多方面的共鸣。坡所倡导的使灵魂升华的"美"，反对道德说教的主张，强调形式美和音乐性，都为后来象征派诗人的创作开先声。坡可被看作是20世纪现代派诗歌的先驱，在描写人与社会的脱节、对周遭环境的厌倦憎恶、与他人的隔阂冷漠、失去自我，和由此产生的变态心理和悲观绝望的虚无情绪方面，现代派作家与坡的创作有许多惊人的相似之处。所以，坡的创作可以说为现代派的文学实践提供范例，而坡的文学创作的意义也正在于此。

雄鹰

阿尔弗雷德·丁尼生 著

导读：

《雄鹰》(*The Eagle*)是英国诗人阿尔弗雷德·丁尼生（Alfred Tennyson, 1808—1892）的一首小诗。初读此诗，呈现在读者眼前的是一只孤傲的雄鹰。诗的第一节刻画静态的鹰，陡峭的山岩、广袤的蓝天、耀眼的日光无不突显出鹰的威风凛凛；第二节描绘动态的鹰，山脚下海浪涌动，山巅上鹰眼犀利，最后鹰之陡然降落更让人措手不及，烘托出鹰的速度之快，并给人以视觉和听觉的双重冲击。该诗虽只有短短六句，但却意蕴无穷。在不同的心境下读此诗会有不一样的体会。

The Eagle

He clasps the crag with crooked hands;
Close to the sun in lonely lands,
Ringed with the azure world, he stands.

The wrinkled sea beneath him crawls;
He watches from his mountain walls,
And like a thunderbolt he falls.

雄鹰曲爪扣危岩,
孑立悬崖日比肩,
身处寰宇倚碧天。

雄鹰脚下海浪涌,
背朝峭壁俯凝瞳,
疾如迅雷海面冲。

爱德华·霍普

《Light Battery at Gettysburg》

过沙洲

阿尔弗雷德·丁尼生 著

导读：

　　短篇抒情诗《过沙洲》（*Crossing the Bar*）是丁尼生年逾八旬在海上写的一首诗，诗行长短交替，形似波浪，诗中含有丰富意象，运用多种修辞手法（暗喻、排比、双关、头韵等）。该诗音韵优美、比喻恰当，且富含意味。诗中表达了一种对待死亡坦然而从容的态度，诗人视死亡为一次优雅、淡定的回家之旅，展示其恬静的宗教信仰。在诗人的葬礼上，来宾朗诵了该诗篇。

Crossing the Bar

Sunset and evening star,
    And one clear call for me!
And may there be no moaning of the bar,
    When I put out to sea,

But such a tide as moving seems asleep,
    Too full for sound and foam,
When that which drew from out the boundless deep
    Turns again home.

Twilight and evening bell,
    And after that the dark!
And may there be no sadness of farewell,
    When I embark;

For though from out our borne of Time and Place
    The flood may bear me far,
I hope to see my Pilot face to face
    When I have crossed the bar.

夕阳西下星辰起,
　　一颗明星召唤我。
当我即将出海去,
　　不把沙洲来侵扰。

愿有如眠般细浪,
　　载我缓缓海中去。
大海深处巨浪掀,
　　潮起潮落归大海。

暮色降临晚钟响,
　　闻声过后夜漆黑!
当我登船扬船帆,
　　别离时分不伤悲。

人生时空虽狭小,
　　潮却载我远海去。
当我绕过沙洲角,
　　盼与领航当面晤。

鉴赏：

　　丁尼生，英国维多利亚时代最受欢迎及最具特色的诗人。他的诗歌准确地反映当时社会上占主导地位的看法及兴趣，这是任何时代的英国诗人都无法比拟的。《民谣及其他诗歌》（1880年）中优美的短篇抒情诗《过沙洲》展示丁尼生的宗教信仰。

　　19世纪晚期和20世纪早期，许多评论家对维多利亚时代的清教主义、一本正经的态度及过多的多愁善感大加批判。丁尼生在其作品中，浓缩了英国中产阶级的各种偏见及道德主张。评论家们经常忽视他的创作技巧和雄辩的口才，过度强调他一味媚俗、过分拘谨及肤浅的乐观主义等缺点。20世纪中叶，评论家们对丁尼生重新评价，既认可他诗歌好的方面，也讨论了他的缺点。他的短篇抒情诗异常精彩，对英国风土人情、自然景色等的描写十分出色。

夜里相会

罗伯特·布朗宁 著

导读：

　　罗伯特·布朗宁（Robert Browning，1812—1889），维多利亚时期代表诗人之一，其主要作品有《戏剧抒情诗》《指环与书》《巴拉塞尔士》等。他与丁尼生作为维多利亚时代两大诗人而齐名。布朗宁以精细入微的心理探索而独步诗坛，对英美20世纪诗歌产生重要影响。《夜里相会》(Meeting at Night)这首小诗分为上、下两小节，每节各6行，上节以描写大海、大地、月亮、沙滩等自然美景开启，下节描写一对情侣夜里海边相会时的细微动作以及内心体验。该诗abccba的韵脚排列方式别具一格。

Meeting at Night

I

The gray sea and the long black land;
And the yellow half-moon large and low;
And the startled little waves that leap
In fiery ringlets from their sleep,
As I gain the cove with pushing prow,
And quench its speed i' the slushy sand.

II

Then a mile of warm sea-scented beach;
Three fields to cross till a farm appears;
A tap at the pane, the quick sharp scratch
And blue spurt of a lighted match,
And a voice less loud, through its joys and fears,
Than the two hearts beating each to each!

一

灰色大海与狭长黑土地；
硕大黄色半月空中低挂；
小小波浪睡中受惊胆怯，
从而在火红卷发中跳跃，
我推船头驶入湿滑泥沙，
降速停船来到小海湾里。

二

一里沙滩飘满温馨海香；
穿三片田直到农场出现；
敲一下窗接着快速刮擦，
擦亮火柴绽放一朵蓝花，
一声低语所露惧色、欢颜，
不及彼此心跳砰砰作响！

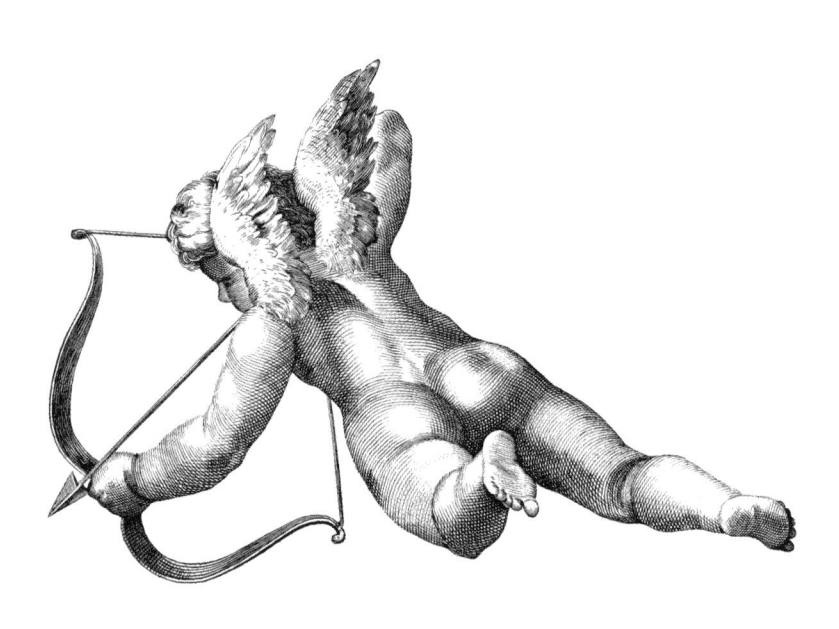

图片来源：PIXABAY

早上分别

罗伯特·布朗宁 著

导读：

布朗宁的《早上分别》(*Parting at Morning*)这首短诗，在强调文本细读、注重结构与语义分析的新批评主义者眼里，堪称一首经典之作。它与布朗宁的另一首短诗《夜里相会》都属情诗，两者合二为一，所以就有相同的韵脚、节奏、诗体、风格以及彼此呼应的语气。

Parting at Morning

Round the cape of a sudden came the sea,
And the sun look'd over the mountain's rim:
And straight was a path of gold for him,
And the need of a world of men for me.

绕过海角大海突然来到,
太阳远眺那座山的边缘:
黄金小路为他笔直伸延,
我需要回到凡尘的俗世。

爱德华·霍普

《Night Shadows》

我已故的公爵夫人

罗伯特·布朗宁 著

导读：

　　《我已故的公爵夫人》(*My Last Duchess*)是布朗宁最具代表性的戏剧独白诗，全诗由公爵对来宾介绍亡妻画像展开，言语中饱含他对已故夫人的抱怨和指责，呈现给读者公爵及公爵夫人两个性格特征存在鲜明对比的人物：心胸狭隘、骄傲自大，残忍专横、嫉妒贪婪的公爵；天真、纯洁和善良的公爵夫人。该诗主要揭示的不是文艺复兴时期的婚姻或审美观，而重在暴露公爵这一人物的本性，引发读者对这位自负自私公爵的批判以及对纯真夫人的同情。

My Last Duchess

That's my last Duchess painted on the wall,
Looking as if she were alive. I call
That piece a wonder, now: Fra Pandolf's hands
Worked busily a day, and there she stands.
Will't please you sit and look at her? I said
'Fra Pandolf' by design, for never read
Strangers like you that pictured countenance,
The depth and passion of its earnest glance,
But to myself they turned (since none puts by
The curtain I have drawn for you, but I)
And seemed as they would ask me, if they durst,
How such a glance came there; so, not the first
Are you to turn and ask thus. Sir, 'twas not
Her husband's presence only, called that spot
Of joy into the Duchess' cheek: perhaps
Fra Pandolf chanced to say, 'Her mantle laps
Over my lady's wrist too much,' or 'Paint
Must never hope to reproduce the faint
Half-flush that dies along her throat.' Such stuff
Was courtesy, she thought, and cause enough

墙上这画是我已故公爵夫人，
她看似像活着一般。我如今
称其为奇迹：潘道夫①师手里
画笔整日忙，使她在此站立。
你不愿坐下看她？我故意说：
潘道夫，因像你一样的生客，
从未读懂画中绘的那副面容，
那份认真注视的深邃和激情，
可他们都转向我（因除我外，
无人为你把拉上的画帘拉开）
可似乎想问我可又不敢发问，
肖像中怎么来的她如此眼神？
你并非第一人回头这样问我。
先生，不只是她丈夫的出现，
使公爵夫人面带笑颜。可能
潘道夫偶尔说过：夫人披风
遮住她手腕太多。或者还说：
隐约的红晕沿颈部渐渐隐没，
绝非画家指望颜料将其复制。
这番大力称赞让她害羞不已，

For calling up that spot of joy. She had
A heart—how shall I say?—too soon made glad,
Too easily impressed; she liked whate'er
She looked on, and her looks went everywhere.
Sir, 't was all one! my favour at her breast,
The dropping of the daylight in the West,
The bough of cherries some officious fool
Broke in the orchard for her, the white mule
She rode with round the terrace—all and each
Would draw from her alike the approving speech,
Or blush, at least. She thanked men,—good! but thanked
Somehow—I know not how—as if she ranked
My gift of a nine-hundred-years-old name
With anybody's gift. Who'd stoop to blame
This sort of trifling? Even had you skill
In speech—which I have not—to make your will
Quite clear to such an one, and say, 'Just this
Or that in you disgusts me; here you miss,
Or there exceed the mark'—and if she let
Herself be lessoned so, nor plainly set
Her wits to yours, forsooth, and made excuse—
E'en then would be some stooping; and I choose
Never to stoop. Oh, sir, she smiled, no doubt,
Whene'er I passed her; but who passed without
Much the same smile? This grew; I gave commands;

足以唤起笑颜。她有一颗心——
怎么说呢？——取悦她快得很，
她太易感动，看什么都喜欢，
且她的目光也喜欢四处观看。
先生，她看啥都一样！胸佩
我送她的赠品，夕阳的余晖，
看某个爱管闲事傻瓜园中折
送她一枝樱桃，还看她骑着
绕行花圃的白骡——所有一切，
一定都会让她同样称赞叫绝，
或红光焕发。她道谢，好的！
可她的感谢——我不知是怎么，
——似把我赐她九百年的名字
与他人的赠品并列。谁愿意
屈尊谴责这无聊之举？即便
你有口才（我没有）使你愿
给这样的人说清楚：你这里
或那里令我厌恶。这有所失，
而那超越界限。即使她肯听，
你这样教训她，她显然不争，
也不挖空心思找借口，真的，
这有失其身份，所以我选择
不屈尊。哦，先生，我走过
她就微笑；可谁走过不收获
她同样多的微笑？事已至此，

211

Then all smiles stopped together. There she stands
As if alive. Will't please you rise? We'll meet
The company below then. I repeat,
The Count your master's known munificence
Is ample warrant that no just pretence
Of mine for dowry will be disallowed;
Though his fair daughter's self, as I avowed
At starting, is my object. Nay, we'll go
Together down, sir. Notice Neptune, though,
Taming a sea-horse, thought a rarity,
Which Claus of Innsbruck cast in bronze for me!

我有令：往后一切笑都停止。
她像活人般站那。请你起立，
客人楼下等。我再重复一次：
你主人——伯爵先生出名大方
足以做保证：对于结婚嫁妆，
我的正当理由不能遭到回绝；
如开头声明，他的美丽小姐
是我目标。不，先生，咱们
一同下楼。看这海神尼普顿
驯海马，我想到了一件珍藏，
那件克劳斯[2]为我铸的青铜像！

注释：

①潘道夫：布朗宁虚构的艺术家，通过让公爵不断强调这位"有名的"艺术家，表现公爵意在强调画作的价值，显示公爵的虚伪。

②克劳斯：同潘道夫，为诗人所虚构的艺术家。

鉴赏：

布朗宁，维多利亚时代第二大诗人，在诗歌、绘画、雕塑和音乐方面都有才能。他幼时聪慧，博览群书，喜爱拜伦、雪莱、济慈的诗歌，从少年时期就开始写诗。有批评家指责诗人过分暴露自我意识和主观感情，这使得他寻求新的表现手法，采用戏剧独白的形式写诗。此后他放弃主观抒情方式而采用客观描写和心理分析方法，独树一帜，许多人随而仿效。

布朗宁发展戏剧独白的手法，并用这种形式写出许多出名的诗作，如《我已故的公爵夫人》等，艾略特、庞德、弗罗斯特等当代诗人都吸收了他的戏剧独白手法。在理论上和创作中，布朗宁不停地探讨邪恶，但他对邪恶缺乏真正深刻的理解，因此，他的复杂的诗歌缺乏深度。布朗宁堪称心理描写大师，他受17世纪玄学派诗歌的影响，用形象表达哲理的论述，喜用独特的比喻，有的诗作流于晦涩，因此他在世时诗名不及丁尼生，但当代评论家视布朗宁为现代诗歌先驱之一。

我歌唱自己

沃尔特·惠特曼 著

导读：

沃尔特·惠特曼（Walt Whitman，1819—1892）是美国19世纪杰出的民主诗人。他出身于农民家庭，当过木工、排字工、教师、报纸编辑、职员等，一生创作大量诗歌。他的诗体现美国的民主理想，反映美国独立战争和内战的重大史实。他站在进步的、正义的立场上，热情呼唤资产阶级的民主和自由。尽管他的《我歌唱自己》（*One's-Self I Sing*）是一首短诗，可他还是念念不忘歌颂"民主"和"自由"这两大主题。

One's-Self I Sing

One's-Self I sing, a simple, separate Person;
Yet utter the word Democratic, the word En-masse.

Of Physiology from top to toe I sing;
Not physiognomy alone, nor brain alone, is worthy for the muse—I say the Form complete is worthier far;
The Female equally with the male I sing.

Of Life immense in passion, pulse, and power,
Cheerful, for freest action form'd, under the laws divine,
The Modern Man I sing.

我歌唱自己,一个简单的个体;
不过要唱出"民主"和"大众"这两个词。

我还要从头到脚为身体而歌唱;
不单单只是外貌和大脑值得歌唱——我想说
　　更值得歌唱的是整个身体;
我更要为男女平等而歌唱。

强大的生命有情感,有脉动,有力量,
其愉悦是因为能在神圣法律下自由地行动,
我为现代人而歌唱。

爱德华·蒙克

《Farewell After the Party》

自己之歌

沃尔特·惠特曼 著

导读：

《自己之歌》(*Song of Myself*)是诗人惠特曼的《草叶集》初版的开卷之作。此诗描述"草叶"的形象：自然界最平凡、最普通的草，有广大的生活天地和强劲的生命力量，它在宽广的地方和狭窄的地方都一样发芽，在黑人和白人中都一样地生长。惠特曼认为草是他的形象，他的意向的旗帜，由代表希望的碧绿的物质所织成，他要用如同草一样朴实的语言讴歌祖国和人民。在诗人心中，不朽的草象征不朽的人民、发展中的美国、自由和民主的理想。

爱德华·霍普

《Seven A.M.》

啊，船长！我的船长！

沃尔特·惠特曼 著

导读：

　　沃尔特·惠特曼于1865年亚伯拉罕·林肯总统遇刺后写下这首《啊，船长！我的船长！》（*O Captain! My Captain!*）的诗歌。因为该诗是写来纪念美国前总统林肯的，所以被归为挽歌。诗中的船长即象征林肯，而船象征着美国。电影《死亡诗社》中曾引用过该诗。

O Captain! My Captain!

O Captain! my Captain! our fearful trip is done,
The ship has weathered every rack, the prize we sought is won,
The port is near, the bells I hear, the people all exulting,
While follow eyes the steady keel, the vessel grim and daring;
  But O heart! heart! heart!
    O the bleeding drops of red,
      Where on the deck my Captain lies,
        Fallen cold and dead.

O Captain! my Captain! rise up and hear the bells;
Rise up—for you the flag is flung—for you the bugle trills,
For you bouquets and rib boned wreaths—for you the shores a-crowding,
For you they call, the swaying mass, their eager faces turning;
  Here Captain! dear father!
    This arm beneath your head!
      It is some dream that on the deck
        You've fallen cold and dead.

My Captain does not answer, his lips are pale and still,
My father does not feel my arm, he has no pulse nor will,

啊，船长！我的船长！我们可怕的航程已经结束，
这艘巨轮历经风风雨雨，赢得的战利品曾是我们的追逐；
港口近在咫尺，我听到阵阵钟声，人们都在欢呼雀跃；
而万众的目光追随着稳健的船身，这艘大船冷酷却不胆怯；
 可是，心啊！心啊！心啊！
  鲜红的血液在一滴滴流失，
   甲板上躺着我的船长，
    他浑身冰凉，与世长辞。

啊，船长！我的船长！起来听那钟声回荡；
起来吧——旌旗为你招展——号角为你吹响，
为了你，花团锦簇，丝带飘飞——为了你，岸边人群挤作一团；
人们把你呼唤，人头攒动，脸色突变，神情焦虑；
 船长就在这里！尊敬的父亲！
  你的头部枕在我的臂膀里！
   这是在甲板上的某种梦境：
    你已倒下，浑身冰凉，与世长辞。

我的船长没有应答，双唇苍白，一动不动，
父亲感觉不到我的手臂，脉搏停止，意志全空，

The ship is anchored safe and sound, its voyage closed and done,
From fearful trip the victor ship comes in with object won;
   Exult O shores, and ring O bells!
      But I, with mournful tread,
         Walk the deck my Captain lies,
           Fallen cold and dead.

大船航程已经结束,安然无恙停在泊位,
结束可怕航程,满载战利品之船凯旋而归;
　欢呼吧海岸,敲响吧钟声!
　　可是我,迈着沉重的步履,
　　　在甲板上踱步,那里躺着船长,
　　　　他浑身冰凉,与世长辞。

鉴赏：

惠特曼，美国著名诗人、人文主义者，创造诗歌的自由体（free verse），其代表作品是《草叶集》。该诗集是惠特曼最重要的著作之一，共收有诗歌300余首，是美国文学史上第一部具有美国民族气派和民族风格的诗集。它开创一代诗风，对美国诗坛产生过很大影响。诗歌奔腾壮阔，大气飞扬，豪放不羁；其诗歌使用朴实粗犷的语言，创造出独具一格的自由体，近于口语，节奏鲜明。诗集中的诗歌像是长满美国大地的芳草，生气蓬勃并散发着诱人的芳香。它们是世界闻名的佳作，开创美国民族诗歌的新时代。

《草叶集》选材广泛，内容丰富，里面既有对美国民主自由的歌颂、对农奴制度的抨击，也有对美国壮丽河山和普通民众的热情赞美。总体来看，《草叶集》体现惠特曼时代的"美国精神"，是惠特曼用诗歌记录的美国史。作者在诗歌形式上有大胆的创新，创造"自由体"的诗歌形式，打破传统的诗歌格律，以断句作为韵律的基础，节奏自由奔放，舒卷自如，具有一泻千里的气势和无所不包的容量。

多佛海滩

马修·阿诺德 著

导读：

马修·阿诺德（Matthew Arnold, 1822—1888）的《多佛海滩》（*Dover Beach*）以非同凡响的气度开篇，三言两语定下诗歌的时空与情感基调。诗人或许突然顿悟，光明与黑暗的交替，潮水的涨落，月的阴晴圆缺，人的悲欢离合，皆符合自然规律，不可忤逆。正是这"永久的悲鸣"，令百感交集的诗人想到另一个时空中的索福克勒斯，并从中找到神秘的思想纽带。人通过回到自己的内心世界，顿悟到世界的表象和实质之间存在着巨大差异。

Dover Beach

The sea is calm tonight.
The tide is full, the moon lies fair
Upon the straits; on the French coast the light
Gleams and is gone; the cliffs of England stand,
Glimmering and vast, out in the tranquil bay.
Come to the window, sweet is the night-air!
Only, from the long line of spray
Where the sea meets the moon-blanched land,
Listen! you hear the grating roar
Of pebbles which the waves draw back, and fling,
At their return, up the high strand,
Begin, and cease, and then again begin,
With tremulous cadence slow, and bring
The eternal note of sadness in.

Sophocles long ago
Heard it on the Aegean, and it brought
Into his mind the turbid ebb and flow
Of human misery; we
Find also in the sound a thought,

今夜大海平静。
潮水涨满,月亮不偏不倚
躺在海峡;法国海岸上光影
忽明忽暗;英国悬崖屹立巍然
平静港湾,巨大无比,微光显露。
我来到窗前,呼吸夜晚清甜的空气!
只见,那一长排浪花拍岸处,
大海与洒满皎洁月光的大地相连,
听吧!你能听到潮落时
浪击鹅卵石发出刺耳的轰鸣声,
潮起时浪柱高耸,浪花飞溅,
潮落潮起,潮起潮落,
伴随着颤抖缓慢而有节奏的回应,
带来永久的悲鸣让人心受折磨。

很久以前,
索福克勒斯[①]在爱琴海听过此事,
他把人类不幸起落的那混乱
带入自己的内心;
我们也在此声中找到一种思绪,

Hearing it by this distant northern sea.

The Sea of Faith
Was once, too, at the full, and round earth's shore
Lay like the folds of a bright girdle furled.
But now I only hear
Its melancholy, long, withdrawing roar,
Retreating, to the breath
Of the night-wind, down the vast edges drear
And naked shingles of the world.

Ah, love, let us be true
To one another! for the world, which seems
To lie before us like a land of dreams,
So various, so beautiful, so new,
Hath really neither joy, nor love, nor light,
Nor certitude, nor peace, nor help for pain;
And we are here as on a darkling plain
Swept with confused alarms of struggle and flight,
Where ignorant armies clash by night.

在这遥远的北海边聆听这一声音。

忠诚的大海
也曾四处横流,椭圆地球的海滨
像一条明亮的腰带卷起褶皱。
可是现在只听见
撤退的悠长哀鸣之音。
撤退,以便去呼吸
那股晚风,撤到地球上的那片
辽阔的岸边和石裸的海滩。

啊,亲爱的,让我们真诚相待!
因为躺在我们面前的这个世界恰似
一方充满梦幻的土地——
如此无常,如此新颖,如此光彩,
却真的没有爱情,没有光明,没有快乐,
没有保障,没有和平,没人帮忙疗伤;
我们就像在一片黑暗的平原上,
打斗和射击的混杂警报声空中响过,
无知的军队在黑夜中交锋肉搏。

注释:

①索福克勒斯:雅典的悲剧作家之一。

鉴赏：

　　阿诺德，英国近代诗人、教育家，评论家，任牛津大学诗学教授长达十年。他主张诗要反映时代的要求，需有追求道德和智力解放的精神。其诗歌和评论对时弊颇为敏感，并能做出理性的评判。代表作有《多佛海滩》等。其诗歌灵感来自古希腊作家，以及歌德、华兹华斯，写过大量文学、教育、社会问题的随笔，猛烈抨击英国生活和文化方面的地方主义、庸俗风气、功利主义，成为当时知识界的批评之声，影响艾略特、利维斯等一代文人。阿诺德的诗歌创作主要集中在19世纪50年代，其诗作主要收集在《诗集》《诗歌二集》和《新诗集》中。

我是无名之辈！你是谁？

艾米莉·狄金森 著

导读：

  美国著名女诗人艾米莉·狄金森（Emily Dickinson，1830—1886）的《我是无名之辈！你是谁？》（*I'm Nobody! Who Are You?*）这首小诗简单却寓意深刻，它就像是狄金森自我的真实写照："当——名人——多么令人厌烦！/像只青蛙——又有什么不同——/将它的名字——在漫长六月——告诉一片正仰慕它的沼泽！"确实，在诗人看来，做公众人物令人厌恶。因此做一个小人物，过平淡而幸福的生活，又有什么不好呢？

I'm Nobody! Who Are You?

I'm Nobody! Who are you?
Are you—Nobody—Too?
Then there's a pair of us!
Don't tell! they'd advertise—you know!

How dreary—to be —Somebody!
How public—like a Frog—
To tell one's name—the livelong June—
To an admiring Bog!

我是无名之辈！你是谁？
你——也是——无名之辈？
那么我们就成一对！
别声张！他们会传——你知道！

当——名人——多么令人厌烦！
像只青蛙——又有什么不同——
将它的名字——在漫长六月——
告诉一片正仰慕它的沼泽！

埃里克·吉尔

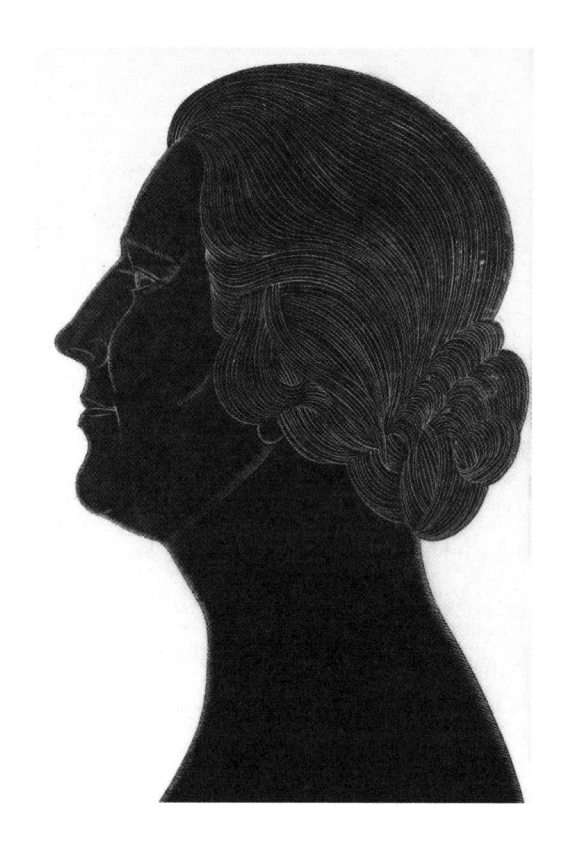

《Xenia Noelle Lowinsky》

这是我给世人的信

艾米莉·狄金森 著

导读：

《这是我给世人的信》(*This Is My Letter to the World*)是狄金森内心的独白，也是她留给世人的赠言，更是一个孤寂的灵魂对未来的期许。诗人将自己用心写就的一首首小诗，当作写给世人的一封封情书。可是，那些吝啬的世人却从未给她回过信，哪怕是只言片语。狄金森的诗大多描述大自然和自己的复杂内心，十分清新自然，所以她说"大自然庄严而温馨/告知简单消息"；她从大自然传递给她的"简单消息"中，汲取源源不断的素材，这就是她高于常人的地方。

This Is My Letter to the World

This is my letter to the World,
That never wrote to Me—
The simple news that Nature told—
With tender Majesty.

Her Message is committed
To Hands I cannot see;
For love of her—Sweet—countrymen—
Judge tenderly—of me!

这是我给世人的信,
世人从未回致——
大自然庄严而温馨——
告知简单消息。

她的信息已经送到
我难见的双手;
为了她——亲爱的——同胞——
请温柔——评价我!

爱德华·蒙克

《游廊上的女人》

我死时听苍蝇嗡叫

艾米莉·狄金森 著

导读：

在狄金森的《我死时听苍蝇嗡叫》(*I Heard a Fly Buzz—When I Died*)这首诗中，诗人写到，当她死时，一切都归于寂静，她的呼吸渐渐变得急促，等待着上帝的降临，可是，就在这个时候，有个意想不到的东西出现了——苍蝇。它出现在诗人和光之间，然后掩盖整个光明。诗中的死亡丝毫无痛感，但是死亡的幻觉确实是阴森的。表面是一个普通的、毫无意义的苍蝇，与我们毫不相关，但是在诗的结尾，它却有了可怕的含义。

爱德华·霍普

《Ground Swell》

说出全部真理而不直说

艾米莉·狄金森 著

导读：

  有时我们因为说话太直接，结果让自己明明是正确的观点和主张不为他人所接受。细想起来，这也不无道理。我们灌输给他人的真理，哪怕放诸四海而皆准，如果可能动摇他们心目中原来就被视为"金科玉律"的信仰和教条，那么，确实让人一时很难接受。于是，诗人狄金森在她的《说出全部真理而不直说》（*Tell All the Truth but Tell It Slant*）这首小诗中告诉我们：说理的成功有赖婉转。

Tell All the Truth but Tell It Slant

Tell all the truth but tell it slant—

Success in Circuit lies

Too bright for our infirm Delight

The Truth's superb surprise

As Lightning to the Children eased

With explanation kind

The Truth must dazzle gradually

Or every man be blind—

说出全部真理而不直说——
成功有赖婉转把握
脆弱感官难耐真理光芒
因为真理惊心动魄
像消除小孩对闪电惊恐
循循善诱解释情形
真理也必渐渐释放光芒
否则人会因此失明——

My Life Closed Twice before Its Close

MY life closed twice before its close—
It yet remains to see
If Immortality unveil
A third event to me

So huge, so hopeless to conceive
As these that twice befell.
Parting is all we know of heaven,
And all we need of hell.

我临终前已经死过两回，
可是我还是想知道，
不朽的神灵是否要揭开
我第三次死亡面罩？

这两次生离死别的构想，
如此宏大如此无解。
死别是所知天堂的一切，
与所需地狱的一切。

鉴赏：

狄金森，美国传奇诗人，出生于一个律师家庭，青少年时代生活单调而平静，受过正规宗教教育。她从二十五岁开始弃绝社交，在孤独中埋头写诗三十年，留下诗作一千七百余首，生前只发表过七首，其余的都是她死后才出版，并被世人所知。她被视为20世纪现代主义诗歌的先驱之一。

狄金森写诗富于睿智，新奇的比喻信手拈来，顺心驱使各个领域的词汇（日常的或文学的，科学的或宗教的）。她喜欢在诗中扮演不同角色，有时是新娘，有时是小男孩，尤其喜欢用已故者的身份说话。其诗作主要写生活情趣、自然、生命、信仰、友谊、爱情。诗风凝练婉约、意向清新，描绘真切、精微，思想深沉、凝聚力强，极富独创性，其中描写大自然的诗篇在美国家喻户晓，常被选入童蒙课本。痛苦与狂喜，死亡与永生，也都是狄金森诗歌的重要主题。虽然她的诗歌以描写日常生活的普通事物为主，但内容深邃，别具一格。布鲁姆将她与惠特曼并列为英语文学经典的中心，一举确立她与莎士比亚、托尔斯泰并列的伟大文豪地位，受到全世界文学界的敬仰。

黑暗中的鸫鸟

托马斯·哈代 著

导读：

托马斯·哈代（Thomas Handy，1840—1928）的名诗《黑暗中的鸫鸟》（*The Darkling Thrush*）创作于19世纪最后一天，即世纪之交的1899年。在这首诗中，诗人表达他那百感交集的心情，和对世纪末的深思。整首诗营造了悲观的氛围，只在最后残留希望的气息。

The Darkling Thrush

I leant upon a coppice gate
   When Frost was spectre-gray,
And Winter's dregs made desolate
   The weakening eye of day.
The tangled bine-stems scored the sky
   Like strings of broken lyres,
And all mankind that haunted nigh
   Had sought their household fires.

The land's sharp features seemed to be
   The Century's corpse outleant,
His crypt the cloudy canopy,
   The wind his death-lament.
The ancient pulse of germ and birth
   Was shrunken hard and dry,
And every spirit upon earth
   Seemed fervourless as I.

At once a voice arose among
   The bleak twigs overhead

我倚在灌木门上边，
　　那时霜呈幽灰，
冬日沉渣使昼之眼
　　虚弱中更孤悲。
那缠藤空中画线痕，
　　若古琴弦断落，
所有出没附近的人
　　皆寻自家炉火。

陆地鲜明轮廓乃似
　　斜卧百年尸体，
其墓室是多云华盖，
　　风为他亡哀泣。
自古来萌发的冲动
　　缩得又干又硬，
地上每个人与我同，
　　似乎都无热情。

忽然头顶有个声音
　　小刺枝间响起，

In a full-hearted evensong
    Of joy illimited;
An aged thrush, frail, gaunt, and small,
    In blast-beruffled plume,
Had chosen thus to fling his soul
    Upon the growing gloom.

So little cause for carolings
    Of such ecstatic sound
Was written on terrestrial things
    Afar or nigh around,
That I could think there trembled through
    His happy good-night air
Some blessed Hope, whereof he knew
    And I was unaware.

黄昏一曲充满真心
　　唱出无限欣喜；
这是只瘦衰老鸫鸟，
　　羽被阵风吹乱，
却选择将灵魂外抛，
　　抛向沉沉黑暗。

远近处任凭我寻搜，
　　在地面万物中，
唱如此欢歌的理由
　　却总遍寻不见。
我可觉那歌声似有
　　无限欢欣喜乐，
夹带让我难以理解
　　他却知的希望。

葛饰北斋

《雪地里的野鸡》

啊,是你正在我的坟上刨?

托马斯·哈代 著

导读:

  托马斯·哈代向来以小说著称于世,可其在诗歌方面却也是成就斐然。其诗作朴实无华,却含意隽永;虽充满对现实的冷眼相看,却富于对生活和爱情的瑰丽幻想,是现实主义与浪漫主义的结合。他的《啊,是你正在我的坟上刨?》(*Ah, Are You Digging on My Grave?*)这首诗以对白式的设计、反复的吟咏和出人意料的结尾向读者展示一幅人情淡漠、世态炎凉的画面。

Ah, Are You Digging on My Grave?

"Ah, are you digging on my grave,
    My loved one?—planting rue?"
—"No: yesterday he went to wed
One of the brightest wealth has bred.
'It cannot hurt her now,' he said,
    'That I should not be true.' "

"Then who is digging on my grave,
    My nearest dearest kin?"
—"Ah, no: they sit and think, 'What use!
What good will planting flowers produce?
No tendance of her mound can loose
    Her spirit from Death's gin.' "

"But someone digs upon my grave?
    My enemy?—prodding sly?"
—"Nay: when she heard you had passed the Gate
That shuts on all flesh soon or late,
She thought you no more worth her hate,
    And cares not where you lie."

"呀,是你在我坟上刨?
　　我爱人?——种芸香?"
——"不:昨天他已去迎娶
一位最聪明富家女。
他说:'我不该话说实,
　　这样不会让她受伤。'"

"那,谁正在刨我坟墓?
　　难道是我亲属?"
——"哦,不。他们静思:'何用!
图何利坟上把花种?
不论如何照料土丘
　　灵魂都已远行。'"

"可有人在我坟上刨?
　　仇敌?——心怀叵测?"
——"不:她听说你入死门,
迟早会与世间离分,
她想你不值她憎恨,

"Then, who is digging on my grave?
    Say—since I have not guessed!"
—"O it is I, my mistress dear,
Your little dog, who still lives near,
And much I hope my movements here
    Have not disturbed your rest?"

"Ah yes! You dig upon my grave ...
    Why flashed it not to me
That one true heart was left behind!
What feeling do we ever find
To equal among human kind
    A dog's fidelity!"

"Mistress, I dug upon your grave
    To bury a bone, in case
I should be hungry near this spot
When passing on my daily trot.
I am sorry, but I quite forgot
    It was your resting place."

无意你处何所。"

"那，谁正在我坟上刨？
　　说吧——我猜不到！"
——"噢，是我，亲爱的主妇，
你的小狗，我还在这，
切望我在此的脚步
　　未将安息侵扰！"

"是啊！你在我坟上刨……
　　何不让早明证
一颗真心为我而留！
遍寻人类所有感情，
终寻不着一种真情，
　　以抵狗的忠诚！"

"女主人，是我坟上刨，
　　只想埋一根骨，
以防每天附近溜时，
我会感觉挨饿忍饥。
抱歉，可是我全忘记
　　这是你安息处。"

Loveliest of Trees, the Cherry Now

Loveliest of trees, the cherry now
Is hung with bloom along the bough,
And stands about the woodland ride
Wearing white for Eastertide.

Now, of my threescore years and ten,
Twenty will not come again,
And take from seventy springs a score,
It only leaves me fifty more.

And since to look at things in bloom
Fifty springs are little room,
About the woodlands I will go
To see the cherry hung with snow.

树最可爱唯樱花，
此时花开满枝挂，
樱树娉立林道旁，
复活时节披素装。

今生在世七十载，
二十韶华不复来，
七十春秋过二十，
只余五十归我使。

观赏花景何其多，
五十春秋无所获，
我欲入林游四方，
望花裹雪挂枝上。

When I Was One and Twenty

When I was one-and-twenty
   I heard a wise man say,
"Give crowns and pounds and guineas
   But not your heart away;
Give pearls away and rubies
   But keep your fancy free."
But I was one-and-twenty,
   Not use to talk to me.

When I was one-and-twenty
   I heard him say again,
"The heart out of the bosom
   Was never given in vain;
"Tis paid with sighs a plenty
   And sold for endless rue.
And I am two-and-twenty,
   And oh, 'tis true,' tis true.

当我二十一岁时，
　　听一智者言语进：
宁献王冠金银币，
　　而别交出你的心；
宁赠珍珠红宝石，
　　莫将真情轻易付。
可惜我才二十一，
　　与我谈此劲白费。

当我二十一岁时，
　　听到智者再次说：
当将真心付出时，
　　时常失去得更多；
往往换来长叹呃，
　　以及无尽之悔恨。
如今我已二十二，
　　惊叹连道此言真。

鉴赏：

霍斯曼，英国著名悲观主义诗人，其田园式、爱国主义、怀旧的创作至今受到英国人的欢迎，著有诗集《什罗普郡一少年》（1896）、《最后的诗》（1922）等。

霍斯曼的诗歌风格独特，他模仿英国民间歌谣，刻意追求简朴平易，使用最简单的常用词营造诗歌的音乐美。其诗内容大多哀叹青春易逝，美景不常，爱人负心，朋友多变，大自然虽美却残酷无情，人生的追求虚幻若梦。诗中有一种刻骨铭心的悲观主义，但同时也表现出对受苦受难普通人的同情。

第二次圣临

威廉·巴特勒·叶芝 著

导读：

威廉·巴特勒·叶芝（William Butler Yeats, 1865—1939）的《第二次圣临》（*The Second Coming*）指传统基督教的一种信念：基督会于未来某天重返这个世界，且在伟大的善恶之战消灭旧有文明后，统治这个世界。基督在未来的再生被称为第二次圣临。叶芝的神秘主义美学认为，世界历史以两千年为单位，善恶交替于时代穿插，好时代后紧接坏时代，如此循环。叶芝写这首诗时（1919）正值一战结束之际，爱尔兰正处于动荡中。惨烈的战争似乎预示旧基督文明的终结，而可怕的时代即将来临。

The Second Coming

Turning and turning in the widening gyre
The falcon cannot hear the falconer;
Things fall apart; the centre cannot hold;
Mere anarchy is loosed upon the world,
The blood-dimmed tide is loosed, and everywhere
The ceremony of innocence is drowned;
The best lack all conviction, while the worst
Are full of passionate intensity.

Surely some revelation is at hand;
Surely the Second Coming is at hand.
The Second Coming! Hardly are those words out
When a vast image out of Spiritus Mundi
Troubles my sight: somewhere in sands of the desert
A shape with lion body and the head of a man,
A gaze blank and pitiless as the sun,
Is moving its slow thighs, while all about it
Reel shadows of the indignant desert birds.
The darkness drops again but now I know
That twenty centuries of stony sleep

猎鹰正在螺旋式地飞翔,
已听不到驯鹰者的呼唤;
万物离析中心已难维系;
世界处于无政府之状态,
同时暗淡血潮渐渐扩散,
四处高尚礼节统统消失;
所有佼佼者都缺乏信念,
然而最坏者却狂到极点。

某种天启无疑即将接近;
第二次圣临无疑将接近。
第二次圣临这话音未落,
宇宙生灵冒出巨大影像,
这影像扰乱了我的视线:
沙漠荒地显狮身人面像,
其目光如太阳空洞无情,
正在迟迟缓缓迈步前行,
四周笼罩愤怒小鸟阴影。
黑暗再现而此刻我知道,
两千年的沉睡令人烦恼,

Were vexed to nightmare by a rocking cradle,
And what rough beast, its hour come round at last,
Slouches towards Bethlehem to be born?

它已成为摇篮边的梦魇,
野兽终有其到来的时刻,
缓慢地走向伯利恒①投胎。

注释:

①伯利恒:耶路撒冷南部城镇,根据《圣经·新约》记载,伯利恒城为耶稣基督的出生之地。

爱德华·霍普

《The Camel's Hump》

驶向拜占庭

威廉·巴特勒·叶芝 著

导读：

《驶向拜占庭》(*Sailing to Byzantium*)是叶芝晚年的诗作，也是诗人对生命和艺术的思考和冥想。叶芝用诗剧的形式描写一位古稀老人对生命的感叹。诗人勾勒出象征不朽艺术且颇具神秘色彩的拜占庭形象，表达出要把脱离肉体的灵魂附在代表永恒的艺术品上的愿望，以获得永生。

Sailing to Byzantium

1

That is no country for old men. The young
In one another's arms, birds in the trees,
—Those dying generations—at their song,
The salmon—falls, the mackerel—crowded seas,
Fish, flesh, or fowl, commend all summer long
Whatever is begotten, born, and dies.
Caught in that sensual music all neglect
Monuments of unageing intellect.

2

An aged man is but a paltry thing,
A tattered coat upon a stick, unless
Soul clap its hands and sing, and louder sing
For every tatter in its mortal dress,
Nor is there singing school but studying
Monuments of its own magnificence;
And therefore I have sailed the seas and come
To the holy city of Byzantium.

一

那国度不为老人所享有。
青年人相拥在垂死世代,
树上的鸟儿在放声歌唱;
鲑鱼成瀑布鲭鱼满大海;
飞禽走兽一夏都在赞扬
世中生与死的一切存在。
在那首悦耳乐曲中陶醉,
都忘却不朽的理性丰碑。

二

衰老之人堪称微不足道,
像一件破衣挂在木棍上,
除非灵魂拍手唱出歌调,
衣衫褴褛唱得更为响亮。
虽然没有教唱歌的学校,
却有人研究丰碑的辉煌,
所以我就远涉重洋来到
拜占庭这座神圣的城市。

3

O sages standing in God's holy fire
As in the gold mosaic of a wall,
Come from the holy fire, perne in a gyre,
And be the singing-masters of my soul.
Consume my heart away; sick with desire
And fastened to a dying animal
It knows not what it is; and gather me
Into the artifice of eternity.

4

Once out of nature I shall never take
My bodily form from any natural thing,
But such a form as Grecian goldsmiths make
Of hammered gold and gold enamelling
To keep a drowsy Emperor awake;
Or set upon a golden bough to sing
To lords and ladies of Byzantium
Of what is past, or passing, or to come.

三

智者哦立于上帝圣火台，
犹如壁画上的嵌金雕饰，
请你们从火中旋转出来，
为我的灵魂当歌唱导师。
把我的心耗尽并且捆在
死动物身上为欲望所蚀，
心已经不知它原为何物；
快把我投入永恒的艺术。

四

脱离自然我将再也不会
化身于这自然物品当中，
我只要让希腊的金匠用
金釉与镀金制作出模样，
让昏睡皇帝清醒于王宫；
或将我镶在金枝上吟唱
那古往今来的悠悠世情，
好让拜占庭王公贵妇听。

鉴赏：

  叶芝，爱尔兰诗人、剧作家和散文家，著名的神秘主义者，是"爱尔兰文艺复兴运动"领袖，也是象征主义诗歌的早期代表人物，对20世纪英国诗歌的发展产生过重要影响。他的诗受浪漫主义、唯美主义、神秘主义、象征主义和玄学诗的影响，演变出其独特的风格。他的艺术代表着英诗从传统到现代过渡的缩影。

  叶芝早年的创作具有浪漫主义的华丽风格，善于营造梦幻般的氛围，韵律感强烈，充满柔美、神秘的梦幻色彩。诗中所述人物多为爱尔兰神话传说中的英雄、智者、诗人、魔术师等。同时，这些诗表现忧郁抒情的氛围，笔触颇似雪莱。进入不惑之年后，在现代主义诗人庞德等人影响下，尤其是有了本人参与爱尔兰民族主义政治运动的切身经验，他的创作风格发生激烈变化。这种变化不仅表现在内容上，也表现在措词上，其结果是一种质朴无华、具体的创作风格。诗人更关注精神的意象和细节，所表现的情感也更为明确，更趋现代主义。叶芝后期诗歌的风格更为朴实、精确，口语色彩较浓，多取材于个人生活及当时社会生活中的细节，且多以死亡和爱情为题，以表达某种明确的情感和思考。

雪夜林边小憩

罗伯特·弗罗斯特 著

导读：

《雪夜林边小憩》(*Stopping by Woods on a Snowy Evening*)是美国诗人罗伯特·弗罗斯特（Robert Frost，1874—1963）的短诗。此诗难能可贵之处在于意境含蓄，用语天然，格律严谨。其意境似乎写景，却别有寓意；其格律是抑扬四步格；其韵脚是每段第一、第二、第四行互押，至于第三行，则于次段与第一、第二、第四行相押，到末段又合为一体，四行通押。

Stopping by Woods on a Snowy Evening

Whose woods these are I think I know.
His house is in the village though;
He will not see me stopping here
To watch his woods fill up with snow.

My little horse must think it queer
To stop without a farmhouse near
Between the woods and frozen lake
The darkest evening of the year.

He gives his harness bells a shake
To ask if there is some mistake.
The only other sound's the sweep
Of easy wind and downy flake.

The woods are lovely, dark, and deep.
But I have promises to keep,
And miles to go before I sleep,
And miles to go before I sleep.

想来我知谁家林,
林主虽住此山村,
他却未见我驻马,
以望满林披雪锦。

我之小马定惊讶,
歇脚附近无农家,
一年最黑夜晚里,
丛林冰湖之间夹。

小马摇动身上铃,
问我是否错处停。
轻风吹拂雪漫天,
唯听铃声相呼应。

林暗林深令人羡,
可我还得守诺言,
要赶几里才安眠,
要赶几里才安眠。

歌川广重

《冬》

未选择的路

罗伯特·弗罗斯特 著

导读:

《未选择的路》(*The Road Not Taken*)是弗罗斯特的代表作之一。这首深邃的哲理诗展现现实生活中人们面对重大抉择时的心情。诗人选择一条人迹稀少、布满荆棘的道路,在作出抉择后,同时遗憾"鱼和熊掌不可兼得",只能选择一条路,坚定地走下去,却在多年后的回忆中轻叹遗憾。这首诗朴实无华而寓意深刻。全诗分四节,每节第一、三、四行,第二、五行押韵,节奏中透着坚定又透出遗憾。其韵律优美,读起来让读者感受到优美的乐感。

The Road Not Taken

Two roads diverged in a yellow wood,
And sorry I could not travel both
And be one traveler, long I stood
And looked down one as far as I could
To where it bent in the undergrowth;

Then took the other, as just as fair,
And having perhaps the better claim,
Because it was grassy and wanted wear;
Though as for that the passing there
Had worn them really about the same,

And both that morning equally lay
In leaves no step had trodden black.
Oh, I kept the first for another day!
Yet knowing how way leads on to way,
I doubted if I should ever come back.

I shall be telling this with a sigh
Somewhere ages and ages hence:

黄木林里两条路不同向，
只可惜我不能同时踏入，
行人我在路口久伫彷徨，
低头朝一条路极目远望，
直到路消失在树林深处。

可我却将另一条路选择，
路荒草萋萋却十分幽寂，
兴许会领我去更好之处，
虽然在这两条路上真的
很少留下了行人的足迹。

清晨两条路虽叶落稠稠，
可都已没踩踏痕迹可追。
我呀留第一条路改天走！
可我懂得此路漫无尽头，
恐怕我将再也难以返回。

多年以后我在某个地方，
一声叹将诸多往事回顾，

Two roads diverged in a wood, and I—
I took the one less traveled by,
And that has made all the difference.

林里两条路分不同方向——
我选人迹罕至的路前往，
从此决定我一生的道路。

爱德华·蒙克

《老树》

修墙

罗伯特·弗罗斯特 著

导读：

《修墙》(*Mending Wall*)是弗罗斯特的又一首名诗。诗歌描写一件既平凡又简单的小事——修墙。然而，修墙的后面却蕴含极其深刻的人生主题：人与人之间的相互沟通。从字面上看，诗人讲一堵石墙，而实际上诗人想讲人与人之间相互沟通的障碍——一堵堵有形或无形的隔墙。面对倒塌的石墙，诗中人分析它倒塌的可能原因，试图说明，人间有许多的有形或无形的墙，墙倒塌是因为很多人不喜欢它，不需要它。人们应该解放思想，共同拆除人为的障碍。令人遗憾的是，他终未能让他的邻居觉醒而停止修墙或开始拆墙，因为他的那位邻居深信："好篱促成好邻居。"

Mending Wall

Something there is that doesn't love a wall,
That sends the frozen ground-swell under it,
And spills the upper boulders in the sun;
And makes gaps even two can pass abreast.
The work of hunters is another thing:
I have come after them and made repair
Where they have left not one stone on a stone,
But they would have the rabbit out of hiding,
To please the yelping dogs. The gaps I mean,
No one has seen them made or heard them made,
But at spring mending-time we find them there.
I let my neighbor know beyond the hill;
And on a day we meet to walk the line
And set the wall between us once again.
We keep the wall between us as we go.
To each the boulders that have fallen to each.
And some are loaves and some so nearly balls
We have to use a spell to make them balance:
"Stay where you are until our backs are turned!"
We wear our fingers rough with handling them.

有一样东西它不喜欢墙，
使墙脚下冻结地面膨胀，
日晒下使墙上石块掉落；
让墙开裂双人并肩而过。
猎人打猎又是另一回事：
我得紧随其后不停修补，
他们拆石块不放回原位，
把兔赶出使其难以躲藏，
惹得那一群狗汪汪直叫。
墙缝没人见开裂听响声，
可春天修墙时它已出现。
我告知山那边住的邻居，
约好某日沿墙巡查一遍，
重新垒筑我们之间的墙。
我们沿着墙体各走一边，
将各自的落石搬起垒上。
有些石成块有些近乎球，
我们口念咒语保其稳妥：
待在那儿等我们回头查！
我们搬石至手指变粗糙。

Oh, just another kind of out-door game,
One on a side. It comes to little more:
There where it is we do not need the wall:
He is all pine and I am apple orchard.
My apple trees will never get across
And eat the cones under his pines, I tell him.
He only says, "Good fences make good neighbors."
Spring is the mischief in me, and I wonder
If I could put a notion in his head:
"Why do they make good neighbors? Isn't it
Where there are cows? But here there are no cows.
Before I built a wall I'd ask to know
What I was walling in or walling out,
And to whom I was like to give offense.
Something there is that doesn't love a wall,
That wants it down." I could say "Elves" to him,
But it's not elves exactly, and I'd rather
He said it for himself. I see him there
Bringing a stone grasped firmly by the top
In each hand, like an old-stone savage armed.
He moves in darkness as it seems to me,
Not of woods only and the shade of trees.
He will not go behind his father's saying,
And he likes having thought of it so well
He says again, "Good fences make good neighbors."

这只不过是种户外游戏,
各站一边时我若有所思:
在此没有必要修这堵墙:
他种松木而我种苹果树。
我说我的果树永不越墙,
也不会在松树下尝松果。
他只说好篱促成好邻里。
春天里我心伤地想知道,
我能否让他这样去思量:
好篱笆何能促成好邻居?
难道说这是养牛的地方?
以前修墙我就得问明白,
我要把什么东西来防范,
我是否冒犯谁家的地盘。
有一样东西它不喜欢墙,
我很想说妖魔想让墙塌。
可真不是妖魔要让墙塌
还是让他自己说出口吧。
我见他紧抓石块的上端,
像石器时代武装的野人。
我想他似已进黑暗地盘,
这黑暗皆因森林和树影。
他不琢磨其父所说的话,
却认为父亲的话很在理,
他又说好篱促成好邻居。

The Snow Man

One must have a mind of winter
To regard the frost and the boughs
Of the pine-trees crusted with snow;

And have been cold a long time
To behold the junipers shagged with ice,
The spruces rough in the distant glitter

Of the January sun; and not to think
Of any misery in the sound of the wind,
In the sound of a few leaves,

Which is the sound of the land
Full of the same wind
That is blowing in the same bare place

For the listener, who listens in the snow,
And, nothing himself, beholds
Nothing that is not there and the nothing that is.

人必须以冬天之心
去凝视冰霜和积雪
覆盖住的松树枝条;

而且也必经历寒冷
才能见冰挂的杜松,
和一月阳光普照下

一棵棵粗糙的云杉;
而不去想那风声和
叶声中的万千伤悲,

那是刮满同样的风
之大地传来的声音,
那风在同样的空地

为雪中的听者吹拂,
听者能见实在之物,
也见万物本质实为虚空。

The Emperor of Ice-Cream

Call the roller of big cigars,
The muscular one, and bid him whip
In kitchen cups concupiscent curds.
Let the wenches dawdle in such dress
As they are used to wear, and let the boys
Bring flowers in last month's newspapers.
Let be be finale of seem.
The only emperor is the emperor of ice-cream.

Take from the dresser of deal,
Lacking the three glass knobs, that sheet
On which she embroidered fantails once
And spread it so as to cover her face.
If her horny feet protrude, they come
To show how cold she is, and dumb.
Let the lamp affix its beam.
The only emperor is the emperor of ice-cream.

唤卷大雪茄者过来，
他肌肉发达让他搅动
厨房里几杯厚重凝乳。
让姑娘慢慢穿上她们
常穿的衣服，并让男孩们
用上月报纸包几枝花。
现实最后战胜幻象，
唯一的皇帝现在成为冰淇淋皇帝。

从缺少三只把手
的松木柜里取出那条
她曾绣的扇尾鸽床单，
铺开后遮盖在自己脸上。
若她伸出嶙峋的双脚，
说明冷得说不出话。
让灯照在她身上。
唯一的皇帝现在成为冰淇淋皇帝。

鉴赏：

　　史蒂文斯，美国著名现代诗人，其诗歌题材和形式丰富多彩，从描写性和戏剧性的抒情诗到沉思诗和离题的议论，都显示他对生活和艺术的热爱。他的音乐诗想象力丰富，叙述简练，关注知识的传播，使现实与外观形成对照，强调想象能给生活带来美的心态和好的秩序。他的许多诗作探讨想象与现实的关系。他认为，诗歌是观察世界的最高虚构；现实是朦胧的，捉摸不定的外部世界是无序的，只有通过想象，才能实现人与现实和谐的结合。他还认为，诗人的最高职责是不写表面的现实，要使"非真实"成为真实。诗歌要取代失去权威的宗教，承担改造世界、拯救人类的重任。人类的心灵将与大自然相结合，缔造人间天堂以代替虚无的天上乐园。他反对"为艺术而艺术"，主张努力发挥诗歌的作用。

　　从风格上来看，除诗歌语言富于音乐性，史蒂文斯还惯用无韵诗和短的诗行，节拍长度上多有巧妙的变化，目的是让读者关注其用语而不把精力放在诗歌韵律形式本身。他还喜欢自造词语，有些只是为了达到某种声音效果。

春天与万物

威廉·卡洛斯·威廉斯 著

导读：

《春天与万物》(*Spring and All*)是美国诗人威廉·卡洛斯·威廉斯(William Carlos Williams，1883—1963)创作的一首现代诗。这首诗描写的早春景象，和我们熟悉的传统诗文里柔美、明媚的春天形象不同。诗人笔下的春天虽肮脏杂乱，不能给读者带来感官的愉悦，不是大肆铺展开的春天，可却是蕴涵无限生机、无限可能的春天。它虽不太甜美可爱，依然留着冬天的痕迹，可这正是乡野早春的本来面目。

Spring and All

By the road to the contagious hospital
under the surge of the blue
mottled clouds driven from the
northeast—a cold wind. Beyond, the
waste of broad, muddy fields
brown with dried weeds, standing and fallen

patches of standing water
the scattering of tall trees

All along the road the reddish
purplish, forked, upstanding, twiggy
stuff of bushes and small trees
with dead, brown leaves under them
leafless vines—

Lifeless in appearance, sluggish
dazed spring approaches—

They enter the new world naked,

在通往传染病院的路边
在涌动的蓝天下
从东北方吹来斑驳的
云团———一阵冷风。远处
那荒野上一片片宽阔的泥田
满是起起伏伏的褐色干草。

一滩滩的死水，
参天树木稀疏分布。

沿着这整条路可见
微红微紫、挺拔笔直、开叉多枝的
灌木和小树木料。
木料下带有褐色的枯叶
和无叶的藤蔓——

外表毫无生机，懒散
且茫然的春天即将来临——

它们赤裸裸地进入新世界，

cold, uncertain of all
save that they enter. All about them
the cold, familiar wind—

Now the grass, tomorrow
the stiff curl of wildcarrot leaf
One by one objects are defined—
It quickens: clarity, outline of leaf

But now the stark dignity of
entrance—Still, the profound change
has come upon them: rooted, they
grip down and begin to awaken

天寒，一切尚未确定
尽管它们进入新世界。其四周
刮着熟悉的寒风——

现在这草明天将长成
野胡萝卜叶坚硬的卷曲状
万物逐一得以确定——
小草快长：叶子轮廓清晰可见

可此时在无比尊严的
入口——它们已然
发生巨大的变化：生根，
向下延伸并开始苏醒

皮埃尔·博纳尔
《The Seine at Vernon》

要说的就是这

威廉·卡洛斯·威廉斯 著

导读：

《要说的就是这》（*This Is Just to Say*）是威廉斯的只有两句话的便条诗。全诗共三节，前两节叙述客观事件，最后一节表达主观感受，而最精彩之处在最后两行。"很甜"解释说话者偷吃梅的理由，而"很冰"不仅与上行的"很甜"在语意和句法上形成强烈对比，而且呼应前面的"冰箱"。细心的读者既会替主人原谅偷吃者的行为，也会为其内疚而略感怜悯。

This Is Just to Say

I have eaten
the plums
that were in
the icebox

and which
you were probably
saving
for breakfast

Forgive me
they were delicious
so sweet
and so cold

我吃了
放在
冰箱里
的梅

可能
是你留
的
早餐

见谅
真可口
很甜
也很冰

鉴赏：

威廉斯是20世纪美国最负盛名的诗人之一，与象征派和意象派联系紧密。其文学创作曾受大学时期的好友埃兹拉·庞德和其他意象派作家的影响，同时继承惠特曼的浪漫主义传统，并在诗歌形式方面进行实验，发展自由诗体。他反对感伤主义的维多利亚诗风，坚持"美国本色"，力求用美国本土语言写作，很少用普通读者不熟悉的词汇。他的主要作品长篇叙事诗《佩特森》是当代美国哲理诗的代表作之一。他被称为美国后现代主义诗歌的鼻祖。

威廉斯是个现实味十足的诗人。他不好张扬传统与观念上的东西，不愿意去讴歌欧洲传统和文明，也反对精英意识，认为诗歌必须走出象牙塔回到现实，还认为只有坚持美国本土精神才是他所要追求的艺术道路。他的这种反欧洲传统文化的思想表现在他提倡的"只有新的，才是好的"的美国化诗歌理念，而他的另一名言"没有观念，除非在事物中"，更是高度概括了他的诗歌创作原则：丢弃传统回归生活，用简洁明了的意象表达思想。

海玫瑰

希尔达·杜丽特尔 著

导读：

《海玫瑰》(*Sea Rose*) 是20世纪美国最伟大的女诗人之一希尔达·杜丽特尔 (Hilda Doolittle，1886—1961) 的一首现代诗。她赢得这样的美誉："一个创造出微型宝玉的完美意象派。"然而，她后期大多数重要作品却不归意象派。她的创造性和伟大之处均表现在后期的诗歌和散文中。

爱德华·霍普

《Morning Sun》

山林仙女

希尔达·杜丽特尔 著

导读：

《山林仙女》（*Oread*）是意象派诗歌的经典之作。该诗以其独特的意象、精练的语言、富有乐感的韵律给读者留下深刻的印象。这首诗虽短小，但用词准确简练，绝不拖泥带水；不仅意象明晰，而且感官性强。大海的宽广和松针的锐利形成鲜明的对比；视觉和触觉的描写表现出一幅森林水墨画。

Oread

Whirl up, sea—
whirl your pointed pines,
splash your great pines
on our rocks,
hurl your green over us,
cover us with your pools of fir.

卷起吧,大海——
卷起你尖尖的松树,
将你那棵棵巨松拍溅
在我们的岩石上,
将你的翠绿猛掷向我们,
用你的片片冷杉把我们遮盖。

爱德华·霍普

《Evening Wind》

海伦

希尔达·杜丽特尔 著

导读：

诗中的海伦是宙斯跟勒达所生的女儿，在其继父斯巴达国王廷达瑞俄斯的皇宫里长大。海伦是人间最漂亮的女人。出生时，那些神赋予她可以模仿任意一个女人声音的能力。她和特洛伊王子帕里斯私奔，引发特洛伊战争。请看诗人杜丽特尔的《海伦》(*Helen*)这首诗如何将历史传说与现代形式融为一体。

Helen

All Greece hates
the still eyes in the white face,
the lustre as of olives
where she stands,
and the white hands.

All Greece reviles
the wan face when she smiles,
hating it deeper still
when it grows wan and white,
remembering past enchantments
and past ills.

Greece sees unmoved
God's daughter, born of love,
the beauty of cool feet
and slenderest knees,
could love indeed the maid,
only if she were laid,
white ash amid funereal cypresses.

希腊人无不讨厌
她那洁白脸庞上平静的双眼,
她亭亭玉立时
那橄榄般光泽的透明,
和她那洁白的双手。

希腊人无不痛斥
她那面无血气的微笑,
回想她曾有的魅惑,
及其所犯的种种陋习,
那变得苍白失色的面色,
更让他们恨入心窝。

希腊人漠然看着
诞于爱中的上帝女儿,
她是那个双足冰冷
双膝修长无比的佳人。
要是真心爱慕这位少女,
只有等待她躺下时,
在墓地松柏间化作洁白灰烬。

鉴赏：

　　杜丽特尔，美国诗人、小说家，是意象派的创始人之一。她的诗歌语调平直，意象精准。《海的花园》是她的第一部诗集，表现出她对细节的精准刻画和处理能力。在一些诗作中，她将历史传说与现代形式相结合，如《墙没在倒塌》和长诗《海伦在埃及》。

　　杜丽特尔的诗及其诗学以女性独特体验为思维起点，以自然界生物的孕育为隐喻，提出从"爱欲"到"想象域"再到精神世界的路径，形成其开创性的感性思维图景。她发现链接身体与意识及超意识的隐秘通道，颠覆男性中心主导的理性传统及权威对美学、历史、艺术、精神等诸多问题的成见。

J. 阿尔弗瑞德·普鲁弗洛克的情歌

托马斯·斯特尔那斯·艾略特 著

导读：

《J. 阿尔弗瑞德·普鲁弗洛克的情歌》(*The Love Song of J. Alfred Prufrock*) 是美国诗人托马斯·斯特尔那斯·艾略特（T. S. Eliot，1888—1965）的诗作，写这首诗时，他刚从美国到欧洲，其思想正发生巨变。该诗标志他已完全转向现代主义。诗虽作于诗人23岁时，但风格已非常成熟。全诗用第一人称自述普鲁弗洛克黄昏时穿过大街赴宴去。主人公内心敏感，有理想，有追求，对日益冷漠的工业化不满，却无力挣脱，最终只能怯懦地忍受现实。该诗名为情歌，实为悲歌，是主人公内心挣扎的写照。

The Love Song of J. Alfred Prufrock

Let us go then, you and I,
When the evening is spread out against the sky
Like a patient etherized upon a table;
Let us go, through certain half-deserted streets,
The muttering retreats
Of restless nights in one-night cheap hotels
And sawdust restaurants with oyster-shells:
Streets that follow like a tedious argument
Of insidious intent
To lead you to an overwhelming question...
Oh, do not ask, "What is it?"
Let us go and make our visit.

In the room the women come and go
Talking of Michelangelo.

The yellow fog that rubs its back upon the window-panes,
The yellow smoke that rubs its muzzle on the window-panes,
Licked its tongue into the corners of the evening,
Lingered upon the pools that stand in drains,

那么我们走吧,我和你,
趁着夜幕铺展在天际,
犹如麻醉病人躺在手术台上;
我们走吧,穿过几条行人稀少的街道,
走过便宜的过夜旅店的夜夜焦躁,
人声低语的休憩地点,
和满地木屑和牡蛎壳的饭店。
街街相连像是一场冗长的争议,
带有阴险的目的,
要将你引入一个重大的问题……
哦,别问:"那是什么?"
让我们去做参观者。

房间里女士们来来往往,
谈论着米开朗琪罗。

黄雾在窗玻璃上擦背,
黄烟在窗玻璃上擦鼻抹嘴,
把舌头轻轻舔入夜幕的角落,
徘徊于立在排水沟里的水池上;

Let fall upon its back the soot that falls from chimneys,
Slipped by the terrace, made a sudden leap,
And seeing that it was a soft October night,
Curled once about the house, and fell asleep.

And indeed there will be time
For the yellow smoke that slides along the street,
Rubbing its back upon the window-panes;
There will be time, there will be time
To prepare a face to meet the faces that you meet;
There will be time to murder and create,
And time for all the works and days of hands
That lift and drop a question on your plate;
Time for you and time for me,
And time yet for a hundred indecisions,
And for a hundred visions and revisions,
Before the taking of a toast and tea.

In the room the women come and go
Talking of Michelangelo.

And indeed there will be time
To wonder, "Do I dare?" and, "Do I dare?"
Time to turn back and descend the stair,
With a bald spot in the middle of my hair—

让掉下烟囱的烟灰落在黄雾背上，
滑过阳台突然跳跃起来，
它明白这是一个温柔十月之夜，
绕房子一圈之后进入梦乡。

确实会有时间
看着黄烟沿街滑行，
在窗玻璃上擦背；
会有时间，会有时间
准备一张脸去见你所遇见的脸；
会有时间去杀伐和创造，
会有时间去做一切的工作，
还有时日让你脱身在餐盘上提问；
时间无论你我都有，
在吃片烤面包和饮茶前，
还有时间让你优柔寡断一百遍，
也让你一百次更改你主意。

房间里女士们来来往往，
谈论着米开朗琪罗。

确实会有时间
去诧异："我敢吗？""我敢吗？"
有时间转身走下楼梯，
我的头顶中央显现秃点——

(They will say:"But how his hair is growing thin!")

My morning coat, my collar mounting firmly to the chin,

My necktie rich and modest, but asserted by a simple pin—

(They will say:"But how his arms and legs are thin!")

Do I dare

Disturb the universe?

In a minute there is time

For decisions and revisions which a minute will reverse.

For I have known them all already, known them all:

Have known the evenings, mornings, afternoons,

I have measured out my life with coffee spoons;

I know the voices dying with a dying fall

Beneath the music from a farther room.

So how should I presume?

And I have known the eyes already, known them all—

The eyes that fix you in a formulated phrase,

And when I am formulated, sprawling on a pin,

When I am pinned and wriggling on the wall,

Then how should I begin

To spit out all the butt-ends of my days and ways?

And how should I presume?

And I have known the arms already, known them all—

(她们会说:"他的头发变得多稀!")
身穿晨礼服,硬领子紧顶下巴,
领带多姿端庄,却别一枚简单领带夹——
(她们会说:"可他的胳膊和大腿多细!")
我敢
扰乱这个世界?
一分钟内还有时间
作出一分钟就可推翻的决定和改变。

因为我已知它们这一切,一切已知:
熟悉这夜晚、上午和下午的情形,
我用咖啡匙衡量自己的生命;
我知道在远处房间传来的音乐里
话语声随那渐消的节奏而渐停。
这样一来我该怎么猜测?

而且我已知道那些目光,所有目光都熟知——
那些说着客套话又盯着你看的眼睛,
把我如标本般定在一根根细钉上,
当我被夹在墙上扭动时,
那么我该如何开始将
度日方式的一切残余吐干净?
然后我该如何改变?

而且我已知道那些手臂,知道所有手臂——

Arms that are braceleted and white and bare
(But in the lamplight, downed with light brown hair!)
Is it perfume from a dress
That makes me so digress?
Arms that lie along a table, or wrap about a shawl.
And should I then presume?
And how should I begin?

Shall I say, I have gone at dusk through narrow streets
And watched the smoke that rises from the pipes
Of lonely men in shirt-sleeves, leaning out of windows?···

I should have been a pair of ragged claws
Scuttling across the floors of silent seas.

And the afternoon, the evening, sleeps so peacefully!
Smoothed by long fingers,
Asleep... tired ... or it malingers,
Stretched on the floor, here beside you and me.
Should I, after tea and cakes and ices,
Have the strength to force the moment to its crisis?
But though I have wept and fasted, wept and prayed,
Though I have seen my head (grown slightly bald) brought in upon a platter,
I am no prophet—and here no great matter;
I have seen the moment of my greatness flicker,

戴镯子的白净手臂袒露在外表,
(可灯光下看出长满浅棕色汗毛!)
是从衣衫上飘出的香气
使得我说话离题万里?
那些手臂搁在桌边或裹着披肩。
那么我该做出猜测?
我又该如何开始?

我要说,黄昏时我已走过狭窄的街道,
看到一个个身着长衫倚在窗口的孤独男人
抽烟时从烟斗里升腾的烟雾?……

我应该变成一对粗糙的爪子
急匆匆地穿过寂静的海底。

而且下午和夜晚有如此安详的睡眠!
像被修长手指缓缓抚平,
睡着……疲倦……或者装病,
平躺在地板上,就躺在你我身边。
喝过茶吃过蛋糕和冰淇淋后我就该
有力气把这一刻推向其危险状态?
尽管我哭泣过拒食过,哭泣过也祈祷过,
尽管我见过我的头(变得有点秃)给放盘上端进来,
我不是先知——在此无关紧要;
我看到我的伟大时刻在闪耀,

And I have seen the eternal Footman hold my coat, and snicker,
And in short, I was afraid.

And would it have been worth it, after all,
After the cups, the marmalade, the tea,
Among the porcelain, among some talk of you and me,
Would it have been worth while,
To have bitten off the matter with a smile,
To have squeezed the universe into a ball
To roll it toward some overwhelming question,
To say: "I am Lazarus, come from the dead,
Come back to tell you all, I shall tell you all"—
If one, settling a pillow by her head,
Should say, "That is not what I meant at all;
That is not it, at all."

And would it have been worth it, after all,
Would it have been worth while,
After the sunsets and the dooryards and the sprinkled streets,
After the novels, after the teacups, after the skirts that trail along the floor—
And this, and so much more?—
It is impossible to say just what I mean!
But as if a magic lantern threw the nerves in patterns on a screen:
Would it have been worth while
If one, settling a pillow or throwing off a shawl,

也看到那位终身男仆拿我的外衣在暗笑,
总而言之,我心惊肉跳。

那么这究竟值不值,
喝过酒,饮过茶,尝过果酱后,
推杯换盏间人们谈论你我的时候,
值不值有此情形:
面带微笑把此事认真提起,
把一切塞进一个球体,
将其滚向某个重大的问题,
说道:"我是拉撒路,来自冥界,
回来告诉你一切,我要把一切告诉你。"——
要是有个人把枕头往她脑袋下边掖,
这人该说:"那根本不是我的意思。
不是那个意思,根本不是。"

那么这究竟值不值,
值不值有此情形:
日落路过庭园,经过雨后大街,
读过小说,喝过茶水,穿过及地长裙后——
要说这,还有更多更多的事说出口?——
不可能把我正想表达的意思说出!
可仿佛有盏神奇的灯把我的想法投上屏幕,
值不值有此情形:
要是有个人放只枕头或扔条毛巾,

And turning toward the window, should say:
"That is not it at all,
That is not what I meant, at all."

No! I am not Prince Hamlet, nor was meant to be;
Am an attendant lord, one that will do
To swell a progress, start a scene or two,
Advise the prince; no doubt, an easy tool,
Deferential, glad to be of use,
Politic, cautious, and meticulous;
Full of high sentence, but a bit obtuse;
At times, indeed, almost ridiculous—
Almost, at times, the Fool.

I grow old ... I grow old ...
I shall wear the bottoms of my trousers rolled.

Shall I part my hair behind? Do I dare to eat a peach?
I shall wear white flannel trousers, and walk upon the beach.
I have heard the mermaids singing, each to each.

I do not think that they will sing to me.

I have seen them riding seaward on the waves
Combing the white hair of the waves blown back

然后转向窗户，这人该说，
"那根本不是我的意思，
不是那个意思，根本不是"。

不！我既非哈姆雷特王子，也无意当王子；
我只是个侍从爵士，一个要为皇家出行
充一充数，布一两次场景，
给王子谏言的人；我无疑是件简单的工具，
一个毕恭毕敬、乐于发挥作用的人，
小心谨慎但精明有方；
尽是高谈阔论却稍显迟钝；
有时，确实近乎可笑荒唐——
有时，却近乎一个痴人。

我老了……我老了……
穿裤子还得卷起裤脚。

我要把头发往后分开？我敢吃桃子？
我将身穿白法兰绒裤子漫步于海滩沙石。
我听过美人鱼彼此对唱歌曲。

我心想她们不会为我而唱。

我看见美人鱼乘风破浪游向大海，
风儿把那海水吹得黑白相间时，

When the wind blows the water white and black.

We have lingered in the chambers of the sea
By sea-girls wreathed with seaweed red and brown
Till human voices wake us, and we drown.

也将吹散在脑后的波浪般白发梳理。

我们流连于一间间海宫卧房,
房间由美人鱼用红棕海草装饰,
直到人声唤醒我们,乃至我们淹死。

鉴赏：

艾略特，英国诗人、诗歌现代派运动领袖，其代表作有《荒原》《四个四重奏》等。艾略特曾在哈佛大学学习哲学和比较文学，接触过梵文和东方文化，对黑格尔派的哲学家颇感兴趣，也曾受到法国象征主义文学的影响。1922年发表的《荒原》为他赢得国际声誉，被评论界看作是20世纪最有影响力的一部诗作，被认为是英美现代诗歌的里程碑。1943年结集出版的《四个四重奏》使他获得了1948年诺贝尔文学奖。

艾略特在其早期创作中善于把自己藏匿在诗句背后，不断变换面具和语气。诗中的"我"大多是戏剧人物，不是直抒胸臆的作者本人。但是总的来说他偏爱一种萎靡不振、无可奈何同时又不失幽默的声音。艾略特认为，诗歌创作中有种"想象的秩序"和"想象的逻辑"，它们不同于常人熟悉的秩序和逻辑，因为诗人省略起连接作用的环节；读者应听任诗中的意象自行进入处于敏感状态的记忆中，不必考察意象用得是否得当，最终自然会收到很好的鉴赏效果。表现这种"想象的秩序"和"想象的逻辑"最为充分的，大概就是奠定艾略特现代派领袖地位的《荒原》。

孤（一

爱德华·埃斯特林·肯明斯 著

导读：

爱德华·埃斯特林·肯明斯（e.e. cummings，1894—1962），美国诗人，现代诗歌技巧的实验性探索大师，他的诗歌内容并不背离传统，但对诗歌形式的各种尝试却显得新颖独特。肯明斯有些诗集的题名离奇古怪，诗行参差不齐，在语法和用词上别出心裁，词语任意分割，标点符号异乎寻常。他的许多诗注重视觉形象，故享有"视觉诗"（visual poetry）之美誉，本文所选的《孤（一》[1（a] 就是其"视觉诗"的代表诗作之一。

1（a

1（a

le
af
fa

ll

s）
one
l

iness

孤(一片叶子落下)孤单单

文森特·梵高

《散步：飘落的树叶》

无题

爱德华·埃斯特林·肯明斯 著

导读：

《无题》（Unknown Title）这首诗是由11个英文单词组成的不符合语法规范的句子（in sunlight over and overing a once upon a time newspaper）。诗人故意违反拼写常规，把这些单词分开排列在上下左右，形成边沿，中间留有许多空白，仿佛就是一张旧报纸，其中有的地方破碎，有的地方缺字，更多的地方字迹模糊不清，呈空缺状。

Unknown Title

insu　　　　　nli　　　　　ght
o
verand
o
vering
A
onc
eup
ona
tim
e　　　ne　　　wsp　　　aper

阳　　　　光　　　　　下
翻
飞着
翻
飞着
一
张
曾
破
碎
的　　　　旧　　　报　　　纸

鉴赏：

　　肯明斯，美国著名诗人、画家、评论家、作家和剧作家，1894年出生于马萨诸塞州剑桥的一个书香人家，受教于剑桥拉丁语学校和哈佛大学。他的诗作大都没有标点和大写字母。他擅长创造不同寻常的排字效果和词语组合，常使用俚语和爵士乐的韵律。他一生大约创作2900首诗歌，被认为是20世纪诗歌的一位著名代言人。

　　肯明斯在其诗中对语言进行独特"实验"，是对传统诗歌的大胆革新。他发表的诗歌在署名时总用小写的"e.e.cummings"，而这个最初由于排字工人粗心造成的错误，恰好迎合他追求的新意。肯明斯还自己创造词汇，比如在"mankind"中间加上"un"，创造出"manunkind"这个新词，用来表示残酷的人类。"爱"总是肯明斯诗歌专注的主题和动力。尽管在当时有些超前，但是肯明斯致力于写出20世纪最为优美的，对性爱、神及自然的崇敬和赞美的诗篇。他在自己的诗歌里改革语法、修辞，满足写诗的需要。除在语言上抛弃传统外，他还在书写格式上进行各种试验，利用印刷格式传达自己的情感。肯明斯十分注重语言的视觉效果，利用书写变异（graphological deviation）手法，竭力把形象的美学原则运用到诗中，如著名小诗《l(a》。

第二次远航

哈特·克兰 著

导读：

  哈特·克兰（Hart Crane，1899—1932），又译哈特·克莱恩，美国当代著名诗人，13岁开始写诗，17岁发表第一首诗，1924年发表爱情诗《远航》（*Voyage*），1926年出版第一本诗集《白色房子》（*White Buildings*）。《第二次远航》（*Voyages* II）表现"溺水而死"的主题。该诗以海岸上孩子们嬉闹开始，他们的纯真与大海的凶猛形成对比。岸上到处是残骸碎片，暗示海洋的力量，显示一种精神或道德上的禁锢，一种威胁，将自己交付给大海就是交付给一种无拘无束的力量，是真正的冒险。诗人发出警告，承认海的残酷，自己抛开一切，跃进大海。诗歌最后两句彻底倒装，显示溺亡而没有坟墓。

Voyages II

—And yet this great wink of eternity,
Of rimless floods, unfettered leewardings,
Samite sheeted and processioned where
Her undinal vast belly moonward bends,
Laughing the wrapt inflections of our love;

Take this Sea, whose diapason knells
On scrolls of silver snowy sentences,
The sceptred terror of whose sessions rends
As her demeanors motion well or ill,
All but the pieties of lovers' hands.

And onward, as bells off San Salvador
Salute the crocus lustres of the stars,
In these poinsettia meadows of her tides,—
Adagios of islands, O my Prodigal,
Complete the dark confessions her veins spell.

Mark how her turning shoulders wind the hours,
And hasten while her penniless rich palms

——然而无边的洪水无拘束,
随风荡漾的这伟大永恒瞬间,
身裹锦缎与女水神并驾齐驱,
腆着硕大肚皮随着月亮转向,
嘲笑我们的爱变幻着的形态;

比如这大海的音域为那写满
银白色字句的卷轴敲响丧钟,
因为王权们的举止或善或恶,
所以他们的一次次开庭撕碎
唯有情人双手的那万般虔诚。

圣萨尔瓦多钟响时奔向前方,
那是向橘红色满天星光致敬,
在随风起伏的一品红草原中,
有岛屿的舒缓,啊我的浪子
完成她静脉涌动的黑暗忏悔。

看她的肩膀随着时间在转动,
忽然她分文不值的肥大手掌

Pass superscription of bent foam and wave, —
Hasten, while they are true, —sleep, death, desire,
Close round one instant in one floating flower.

Bind us in time, O Seasons clear, and awe.
O minstrel galleons of Carib fire,
Bequeath us to no earthly shore until
Is answered in the vortex of our grave
The seal's wide spindrift gaze toward paradise.

掠过卷曲泡沫和浪花的题名，
睡眠、死亡与欲望忽成真时，
它们瞬间相拥于一朵大浪花。

分明可怕的季节啊快绑我们。
加勒比火船上的吟游诗人啊，
把我们抛在远离尘世的岸边，
直至在坟墓漩涡中得到回应，
海豹掀起的巨浪凝视着天堂。

鉴赏：

克兰，20世纪美国最重要的诗人之一，受到托马斯·斯特尔那斯·埃利奥特的启蒙。克兰开始写诗时，形式上虽然依循传统，但是在遣词造句上常采用古语。他的诗作尽管时常被批评晦涩难懂、故弄玄虚，可是他却被普遍认为是20世纪最具影响力的诗人之一。其主要作品包括诗集《白色建筑群》《西锁岛：一束岛》，以及长诗代表作《桥》。

镜子

塞尔维亚·普拉斯 著

导读：

塞尔维亚·普拉斯（Sylvia Plath，1932—1963）是继艾米莉·狄金森和伊丽莎白·毕肖普之后最重要的美国女诗人。1963年，她最后一次自杀成功时年仅31岁。这位颇受争议的诗人既因富于激情和创造力流芳百世，又因其与另一位英国诗人休斯情变自杀的戏剧化人生而成为文学界经久的话题。生前，普拉斯只出过一本诗集；去世后，休斯为普拉斯编选几本诗集，奠定她的诗人地位。普拉斯的《镜子》（*Mirror*）是一面镜子的自述，镜子看东西跟人有别，没有先入为主的印象，很诚实，不隐瞒什么，不把人没有的东西强加给人。

Mirror

I am silver and exact. I have no preconceptions.
Whatever I see, I swallow immediately.
Just as it is, unmisted by love or dislike.
I am not cruel, only truthful—
The eye of a little god, four-cornered.
Most of the time I meditate on the opposite wall.
It is pink, with speckles. I have looked at it so long
I think it is a part of my heart. But it flickers.
Faces and darkness separate us over and over.

Now I am a lake. A woman bends over me.
Searching my reaches for what she really is.
Then she turns to those liars, the candles or the moon.
I see her back, and reflect it faithfully.
She rewards me with tears and an agitation of hands.
I am important to her. She comes and goes.
Each morning it is her face that replaces the darkness.
In me she has drowned a young girl, and in me an old woman
Rises toward her day after day, like a terrible fish.

我乃银色且成像逼真,没有任何成见。
无论看到什么,我都立刻吞下。
什么都照原样吞,不为好恶所迷糊。
我并不残酷,只是真实——
一只小天使的眼睛,四四方方。
大部分时间我都对着那墙壁在冥想。
墙呈粉色,带有斑点。我已盯它很久,
我想墙是我内心的一部分,可它却在闪动。
各种面孔和黑暗一次又一次将我们分开。

现在我是一座湖。一个女士俯身于我,
在我的上下搜寻她真实的面容。
然后她转向那些骗子——蜡烛或月亮。
我看她的背影,并如实反映。
她却以泪洗面挥舞双手回报我。
对她而言我很重要。她来回照镜子。
每天清晨就是她那张脸替代黑暗。
在我镜里她淹死一个少女,而一个老妇人
却像一条可怕的鱼儿日复一日朝她浮起。

鉴赏：

　　普拉斯，20世纪美国诗人、小说家，是自白派的代表诗人之一。普拉斯的诗歌具有明显的自白派诗歌的特征，也有自己独特的创作手法和艺术追求。她短暂而悲剧的一生也给她的创作生涯蒙上诗化的色彩。普拉斯的诗歌具有浓厚的黑色艺术特点，她对"黑色"的偏爱使她的许多诗作读起来会有阴沉、压抑之感。她一生迷恋死亡，两次尝试自杀未果，在第三次自杀时结束短暂的生命。然而，普拉斯同时又渴望重生，她在许多诗歌中也表达类似的主题。她的诗作在她生前并没有得到太多的关注，不过人们逐渐发现她这些黑色艺术中的独特魅力，发现她留给世人一个独特的艺术世界。

译后记

英语诗歌浩如烟海，《英美经典诗歌选译》所选诗作，只是沧海一粟。译者在翻译选材时，力求涵盖一千五百年来英诗的辉煌历程，涉及英美诗歌主要流派代表性作家的代表作，经过反复筛选的诗作中，既有现实主义的作品，也有浪漫主义的作品；既有体现古典风格的作品，也有体现现代艺术的作品。诗歌作者既有英美诗人，也有爱尔兰诗人，他们既包括英诗中最伟大的诗人、文艺复兴时期的巨匠莎士比亚，也包括出生于20世纪30年代的美国女诗人塞尔维亚·普拉斯。选诗时考虑到广大初涉英诗领域的读者水平，所选诗歌既有短小精悍的，也有在英美文学史上经久不衰的优秀长诗。

英美诗歌名家写作风格异彩纷呈，译者在翻译过程中，以"忠实"和"通顺"为基本标准，以"形美、音美、意美"为指导原则，力求在保持原诗风貌及其韵律的基础，传达出诗歌优雅的意境，同时，尽可能将作者的风格传达给中文读者。

由于本书翻译任务重，时间紧，难度大，加之译者水平有限，错误与疏漏在所难免，望广大读者批评指正。

福州工商学院文法学院　高　远
二〇二一年十二月
于福州工商学院方广书院